Chance should probably go.

Probably.

But he didn't.

Being a chaplain had hardwired him to be concerned for the sick and the struggling. Rayne was both.

He scowled, pacing back to the window as the doctor continued his examination of Rayne. Outside, sheets of ice fell from the charcoal sky, pinging off the ground and cars, shimmering on trees and bushes. A shadow shifted at the edge of the lot, merged with another shadow. Two figures standing in the icy downpour at midnight with the windchill dipping to twenty below?

Not something any sane person would do, but that didn't mean anything sinister was going on.

Someone was in my room.

Rayne's words drifted through his mind, and he couldn't ignore them or the quicksilver shot of adrenaline that flooded his veins.

Maybe nothing was going on.

Probably nothing was.

But it wouldn't hurt to check things out.

Books by Shirley McCoy

Love Inspired Suspense

Die Before Nightfall
Even in the Darkness
When Silence Falls
Little Girl Lost
Valley of Shadows
Stranger in the Shadows
Missing Persons
Lakeview Protector
*The Guardian's Mission
*The Protector's Promise
Cold Case Murder
*The Defender's Duty
**Running for Cover
Deadly Vows
**Running Scared
**Running Blind
Out of Time
**Lone Defender
**Private Eye Protector

*The Sinclair Brothers
**Heroes for Hire

Steeple Hill Trade

Still Waters

SHIRLEE McCOY

has always loved making up stories. As a child, she daydreamed elaborate tales in which she was the heroine—gutsy, strong and invincible. Though she soon grew out of her superhero fantasies, her love for storytelling never diminished. She knew early that she wanted to write inspirational fiction, and she began writing her first novel when she was a teenager. Still, it wasn't until her third son was born that she truly began pursuing her dream of being published. Three years later she sold her first book. Now a busy mother of five, Shirlee is a homeschool mom by day and an inspirational author by night. She and her husband and children live in Washington and share their house with a dog, two cats and a bird. You can visit her website at www.shirleemccoy.com, or email her at shirlee@shirleemccoy.com.

SHIRLEE McCOY

PRIVATE EYE PROTECTOR

Love Inspired

Recycling programs
for this product may
not exist in your area.

 LOVE INSPIRED BOOKS

ISBN-13: 978-0-373-08285-8

PRIVATE EYE PROTECTOR

www.LoveInspiredBooks.com

Printed in U.S.A.

You are my hiding place;
you will protect me from trouble
and surround me with songs of deliverance.
—*Psalms* 32:7

To my parents Edward and Shirley Porter
who taught me what a lifetime of love looks like.

And to my husband Rodney,
who shows me every day.

ONE

Someone stood in the open door of the room, his silence more compelling than the steady beep of machinery, more alarming than the agonizing pain that had tugged Rayne Sampson from the velvety darkness she'd floated in for…

How long?

She didn't know.

Had no sense of time passing.

She shifted, the mechanized beep jumping with her pulse.

Pain.

In her head.

Her joints.

Someone watching. Time stalling. Nothing

moving. Not Rayne. Not the figure standing near the door.

Get up.

Find Emma.

The command shot through her pain-racked head, and she swung her legs over the bed, trying desperately to figure out where she was, how she'd gotten there.

Where her daughter was.

Emma!

She had to find her, couldn't fail her.

You don't have what it takes to be a mother, Rayne. You're too young. You need to grow up a little, be a wife first. Be my wife. Just like we planned.

Michael's words drifted through her mind, filling her head so that it pounded even harder, throbbed more insistently.

When had he said those things?

A week ago?

A month ago?

She had no sense of time passing, and her heart thundered with the knowledge.

"Where's my daughter?" she asked the man who watched, but the doorway was empty, the hall beyond brightly lit. The sound of footsteps and voices drifted into the room. People chatting and laughing, the sounds echoing through Rayne's pounding skull.

Get up!

She pushed to her feet, nearly tripping over an IV pole.

A hospital.

She was in a hospital.

But she had no idea how she'd gotten there. No memory of an accident or an injury.

"Where's Emma?" she spoke out loud, trying desperately to cling to the thought as darkness edged in and the floor slid away.

Cold sweat beaded her brow, her limbs trembling as she tried to hold on to consciousness.

You don't have what it takes to be a mother.

"You're wrong," she muttered—not sure if she was in the moment or in the past—her voice raspy, her thoughts fuzzy.

Find her.

She took a step and fell into darkness.

Emma!

The name speared through the darkness, and she jerked back to the room, the endless mechanized beeping.

The pain.

Overwhelming, mind-searing pain. Cold tiles seeped through cotton and chilled her to the bone. On the floor, but she didn't know how she'd gotten there.

Footsteps sounded on tile. Close. Coming closer.

The man returning?

She struggled to her hands and knees.

Get up.

Find Emma.

Hurry.

But, her movements were sluggish and un-coordinated, her efforts futile.

"Rayne? What are you doing?" A voice drifted into the darkness, light splashing across the floor, splashing into her eyes and blinding her, making her turn her head to the side, away from the glare.

She blinked, focused.

Boot-clad feet just inches away.

Hands wrapped around her waist, eased her to her feet.

Warm breath against her cheek, and she was being lifted off the ground, the machine beeping, her ear pressed against something warm and solid.

She let her eyes slide shut, relaxing against the touch that felt so safe.

Someone brushed strands of hair from her cheek.

Her brother or father?

Michael?

Couldn't be Michael. She'd given back the ring, broken things off.

"Dad? Jonas?" She wanted to open her eyes, tried to open them, but they felt so heavy.

"Chance."

She forced her eyes open, looked into a stranger's face.

Dark hair, high cheekbones, pale eyes.

She knew those eyes.

Didn't she?

"Who are you?"

"Chance Richardson." He frowned, pressed a button on the bed rail. "We work for the same company. You rent an apartment from my mother. Don't you remember?"

Did she remember?

She tried to pull the information from her mind, found nothing but emptiness and a cold, hard kernel of fear. "I live in Arizona. I work for a women's shelter in Phoenix."

"Do you know what day it is, Rayne?" He looked into her eyes, searching for something, but she had nothing to give. His eyes shimmered blue or green or gray, and she was sure she'd looked in them before.

When?

Where?

"I… No."

"Do you know what city you're in?"

A memory surfaced. Packing the U-Haul, strapping Emma into her car seat, leaving everything she knew to take a new job in a new place. "I remember packing to leave. That's it."

"Do you know where you are?" He pressed the button on the bed rail again, and she knew he was summoning a nurse. A nurse couldn't help, though. All that could help was remembering, and that seemed to be impossible.

"The hospital."

"Do you remember how you got here?"

"No."

"You were in an accident," he said, as if he hoped it would spark a memory.

All it sparked was terror.

Emma!

"Where's my daughter?" Rayne tried to sit up, but Chance pressed her back.

"She's fine. She wasn't in the car with you."

"Thank God." She closed her eyes, the prayer swirling through her mind again and again and again.

"He was definitely looking out for both of you. Do you remember what happened?"

No, and that terrified her.

She tried to respond, but her thoughts were clumsy, her eyelids leaden.

"Do you remember the accident, Rayne?" he persisted, pulling her from the edge of sleep.

She scowled, wondering if she knew him well enough to tell him to go away and leave her alone. Not to ask any more questions, because every question she couldn't answer only added to her fear.

"Do you know how it happened? Where it happened?"

"In my car?" There. Finally something she *could* answer.

"Funny, Goldilocks, but that's not what I mean, and you know it."

"I wasn't trying to be funny, and my hair isn't gold, it's platinum."

"Looks gold to me. Do you know what town you're in?"

That she could answer, too.

She'd left Phoenix to work in Spokane, Washington. If Chance was her coworker, she must be there.

"Spokane, but I'm tired of playing twenty questions, so let's stop for a while, okay?" She opened her eyes, looked into his gray-blue gaze.

Eyes she knew but didn't know.

The world spun, and she spun with it, falling back into darkness so quickly she thought she might never escape it.

She reached out, grabbed something warm and solid.

His hand.

Calloused and rough and oddly familiar.

She knew his eyes, and she knew him, but she had no memory of meeting him, no knowledge of their shared history. How far back did that history go? How much time had passed since her last memory?

Was Emma still a baby?

Had she grown into a toddler?

Something more?

Terrified, she sat up, stars shooting in front of her eyes.

"I need to see my daughter." The frantic edge to her voice matched her racing pulse and the frenzied beep of the machine.

"Calm down, Rayne. Emma is fine. My mom was babysitting her while you worked, and she's still taking care of her." Chance pressed a palm to her cheek, forced her to look into his eyes.

Calm.

Confident.

Not panicked at all.

Then again, he wasn't the one with amnesia.

"Is everything okay in here?" A nurse walked into the room, her dark eyes widening as she saw Rayne. "You're awake. How are you feeling?"

"Aside from having a splitting headache and amnesia? Okay."

"Amnesia? The nurse looked at chance, and he nodded.

"She seems to be missing her recent memories. No idea what day it is, no memory of the accident. She doesn't seem to remember me or the area."

"She's sitting right here, and she can speak for herself," Rayne grumbled, but throbbing pain stole the heat from her words, and she really didn't have the strength to add to what he'd said.

Besides, what would she add?

He'd said it all.

All her recent memories were gone. Trying to find them was like searching through a sea of nothingness.

"I'll page the attending physician. He'll want to ask you a few questions, Rayne. In the meantime, on a scale of one to ten, what's your pain level?"

"Seven." But, compared to her fear and confusion, that was negligible.

She wanted to remember everything. Wanted it with a desperation that made her physically ill.

"When the doctor comes in, we'll see if you can take something for that."

"I don't need anything for the pain. All I want is to go home and see my daughter." Only she didn't know where home was. Didn't know where her daughter was.

Being a parent is a big responsibility. Let

someone else take it on. Someone who really wants a baby.

Michael spoke from the past, and Rayne realized she'd closed her eyes, was drifting on waves of distant memories.

Or maybe not so distant.

"What day is it? What's the date?" she asked.

"Friday, November 28th, 2011." Chance answered, smoothing a lock of hair from her forehead.

She'd left Phoenix at the beginning of October. That meant she'd lost nearly two months of her life. Two months of Emma's life.

Better than the alternative.

Better than years or decades.

"I need to see Emma." She sat up, ignoring the nurse's protest, ignoring Chance's hand pressed to her shoulder.

Michael had been wrong.

Everything he'd said, everything he'd believed about her ability to parent Chandra's baby had been wrong.

Rayne had spent the past eight months proving that.

She wouldn't fail now. Wouldn't leave her baby with a complete stranger.

"Do you really think you're going to do her any good in the condition you're in?"

"I'll do her a lot more good if I'm with her than if I'm away from her."

"My mother has been her babysitter since you moved into the apartment. She and Emma will do just fine together. All you need to worry about is getting better," Chance said, and Rayne reached for a name, a face, something to go with his words.

Nothing.

Blank.

"I don't know your mother. I don't know you." Her breath came in short gasps, and she felt helpless to control it. Panic edged out everything. The nurse. Chance. The pain that slammed through Rayne's skull.

"You're not going to fall apart, Rayne. You have a kid to get home to and a life to live. This is just a blip on the radar, so take a deep breath and pull yourself together," Chance growled, his eyes blazing into hers, forcing her back from the brink.

She wasn't sure whether she wanted to thank him or punch him, but his harsh words had worked. She could breathe. She could think.

"Easy for you to say. You're not the one with holes in your memories."

"That's better, Goldilocks." He patted her hand, moved aside as the nurse leaned in to take Rayne's vitals.

"Partial amnesia is very common with head injuries. Give yourself a little time. Things will come back to you." The nurse jotted something on Rayne's chart, offering an easy smile.

"When?"

"Unfortunately, it isn't an exact science. Sometimes, memories come back quickly. Sometimes, it takes months. Even years."

"I want them back *now*. I can't stomach the thought of my daughter with someone I don't know," she said, the words blurting out before she thought about how they'd sound.

"Of course you feel that way. What mother wouldn't? But I can assure you that Lila Richardson is one of the most wonderful women around. She'll take good care of your daughter."

"You know her?"

"She taught my Sunday school class when I

was a kid, and now, she teaches my son. She's great, and I'm not just saying that because Chance is in the room."

"That make me feel better." But not much. Emma was her responsibility. She'd made a promise to Chandra, and she didn't take that lightly.

Sure, I'll raise her if something happens to you.

But she hadn't expected anything to happen to her best friend. Hadn't thought very hard about what it would mean to take on the responsibility of raising another human being.

"Good. Now, you just rest for a while, okay? The doctor should be in shortly. Hopefully, by midnight, you'll have some pain medicine and be fast asleep. Everything will look better in the morning." The nurse pulled the blanket up to Rayne's chin, tucked it around her shoulders.

Everything is going to be okay." Chance said, his words soothing and smooth, commanding her attention.

"Okay? I'm missing nearly two months of my life."

But maybe the nurse was right.

Maybe things *would* look better in the morning.

Still, something nagged at the back of her mind, something that shivered along her spine, lodged at the base of her skull, pounded into her consciousness.

Someone standing in the open doorway, watching.

Chance?

A doctor?

Did it matter?

People came and went in hospitals. There was nothing alarming about that, but she couldn't shake her fear, couldn't put the image out of her mind.

A man.

Watching.

"Were you in my room earlier, Chance?" she asked, because she had to know. Couldn't rest until she was sure.

"I've been waiting down in the emergency room while they got you settled. My mom was here with Emma, but Emma got fussy and they had to leave. I walked them out to the parking lot and came up. Why?"

"Someone was here, standing in the doorway, watching me."

"The cleaning crew just made its rounds. You probably saw one of the team," the nurse interjected.

A custodian?

Rayne didn't think so.

But her head had been fuzzy, her thinking muddled, her vision blurred.

The nurse glanced at her watch. "I need to go do rounds. The doctor will be here soon. If you need anything before then, just buzz."

She hurried out of the room.

"Are you okay?" Chance asked, and she shrugged, her shoulders aching, muscles she hadn't even realized she had throbbing in protest.

A car accident.

Amnesia.

Of course she was seeing danger in the shadows...and the doorways.

"I will be."

"Then why do you look so scared?" He studied her face, searched her eyes, saw more than she wanted anyone to.

Mothers were tough, right?

Strong.

Immovable.

They didn't rely on other people, because they didn't need anyone to take care of them. They took care of themselves.

So no more relying on other people for Rayne.

That was rule number one for heart-healthy living, and Rayne planned to remember it. No matter what else she forgot.

"I'm not scared. I just don't think the guy I saw was a custodian."

"Then who do you think he was?"

"I don't know."

"He could have been a nurse or a doctor."

"Maybe."

"Look, if you're nervous about staying here alone tonight…"

"I'm not." At least, not very.

"I can stay with you."

"Really. I'll be fine."

But something nagged below the surface of her mind.

Bright lights. Terror.

There and gone so quickly she couldn't hold on to them.

"I planned to hang out for a while anyway, so I'll wait until the doctor comes in. Then I'll talk to the maintenance staff. See if any of them were in your room. How does that sound?"

"It sounds like you're placating me."

"I don't have the time or patience to placate anyone, Rayne." Chance stretched his long, muscular frame, his gray-blue gaze never leaving her face.

Handsome.

Really handsome.

How could she not remember a face like his?

"You said we work for the same company."

"That's right. I'm a private detective with Information Unlimited. You've worked with several of my clients."

A new job.

A new life.

A fresh start.

Working as a victim's advocate for the P.I. firm that employed her sister-in-law had seemed like a perfect opportunity to put her mistakes behind her.

That she remembered.

She also remembered her mistakes.

Mistake.

One mistake.

But a big one. Thankfully, she'd called her engagement off before it could turn in to a catastrophe.

Something buzzed, the sound jerking her out of the half sleep she'd fallen into. She sat up straight, her heart pounding. Dizzy, disoriented.

"It's just my phone," Chance said quietly.

Still there.

Still handsome.

Still a stranger.

She watched as he answered his phone, studying his face, trying to remember the day they'd met, the place.

"Yes. She's awake. Seems fairly lucid, but she has partial amnesia." His words penetrated the thick fog in her brain, and she frowned.

"I'm completely lucid."

"Did you hear that?" he asked, then nodded. "I think so. Let me check. Are you up to talking to your brother?"

"Jonas?"

Of course Jonas.

She only had one brother.

Maybe she wasn't as lucid as she'd thought.

"Yes."

"Sure." She took the phone, pressed it to her ear, her hand shaking. "Jonas?"

"Hey, sis. Rough night, huh?" His familiar voice brought unwanted tears to her eyes, and she sniffed them away.

"I've had better."

"You okay?"

"Aside from a headache, I'm fine."

"Glad to hear it. We've been worried, but there aren't any flights leaving until tomorrow afternoon. We should be there sometime tomorrow night."

"We?"

"Skylar and me. Mom and Dad."

"You can't drop everything you're doing to fly out here."

"Sure we can."

"Maybe I should rephrase that. I'm doing great. By tomorrow, I'll be home and back to my routine. I'd rather you all come up for Emma's first birthday. Just as we planned."

"There's no reason why we can't come now and in April."

"It's too expensive, and I'll spend the whole time you're here feeling guilty."

"Rayne—"

"I promise—if I need you guys here, I'll let you know. But for right now, I'm fine."

"Chance said you have partial amnesia. I don't consider that fine."

"There are just a few holes in my memory. The nurse said that's common with head injuries. I'll probably remember everything before I leave the hospital."

Chance snorted at her optimism, but Rayne ignored him.

She loved her family, but they worried too much, jumped in to rescue her before she ever had an opportunity to rescue herself. When she'd taken custody of Emma, Rayne's mother had offered free babysitting and had insisted on cooking meals, doing the laundry and cleaning. After Rayne broke up with Michael, Jonas and Skylar had traveled from New Mexico to Arizona and stayed with her for a week. The day she'd been held at gunpoint…

She frowned.

No need to go back there.

She'd made her decision before that, knew that she had to break away, prove herself as a mother on her own. No parents and siblings stepping in to rescue her, no fiancé telling her she wasn't capable. Just Rayne and Emma making a wonderful life in a beautiful new town.

Anything else would mean weakness, anything else could lead to heartache.

And she didn't want either of those things in her life.

"All right. It's your choice, but I'm not going to say I'm happy about it. You'll call if you need anything, right?" Jonas asked, and she forced herself to focus on the question, on the conversation.

"You know I will."

"I'll call Mom and Dad and let them know you're okay, but as soon as you get a chance, give them a ring. Mom has been beside herself since she got the call saying you were in the hospital."

"I'm really sorry I worried all of you."

"That's what families are for."

"Worry?"

"Something like that. Keep safe, sis. Love you." Jonas disconnected and Rayne handed the phone back to Chance.

"So you really think you're going back to

your normal routine tomorrow?" he asked as he shoved the phone in his pocket.

"I don't see why not."

"Let's start with the fact that you're lying in a hospital, hooked up to an IV, with a lump the size of a grapefruit on the side of your forehead."

"Is it really that big?" She fingered the bump on her forehead, wincing as she probed the tender flesh.

"I might be exaggerating, but my point is the same. You're not going to be doing anything but resting tomorrow."

"Hopefully, with my memories intact." Her words were slurred, her mind fuzzy and, for a moment, she wasn't sure what they were talking about. Why they were discussing it.

Didn't even know if she cared.

"You're drifting off again, Goldilocks."

"Just resting my eyes," she mumbled.

"Good. I'll be back in a few minutes." Fabric rustled, and she knew he was going to leave. Felt sure that if he did, something bad would happen. Nothing about this place was familiar, except for him. His eyes. The warmth of his hand. And she didn't want to be left alone in the dark again without either one.

"Don't go." She grabbed his hand, looked into his face. Familiar and strange all at the same time.

"Okay." He settled back into the chair. No question about why she wanted him there. No hesitation. No list of things he needed to do.

Just his presence, given without reservation.

Not something she was used to.

Not something Michael would have done.

Michael.

Funny that a stranger was willing to give more of himself than her fiancé ever had.

Or maybe not so funny.

Michael had promised her everything, but he'd given her nothing of consequence. Dinner dates were nice, phone calls on Tuesday afternoons were fine, but when push came to shove, he'd proven he couldn't be counted on.

If you insist on playing mother to a drug addict's baby, then we're through. Are you willing to let that happen, Rayne? Willing to give up what we've spent almost three years building?

She'd been willing.

She wasn't sure she'd been ready to be a mother, though.

Still, she didn't regret the promise she'd made the day Chandra had given birth to the red-faced, red-haired infant.

Even then, Rayne had loved Emma. She just hadn't realized she would be her mother.

She was, though, and she'd do whatever it took to raise her, protect her and give her the life Chandra would have wanted for her.

It was the last thought she had before darkness carried her away.

TWO

Holding hands with Rayne Sampson was not how Chance had planned to spend his evening. As a matter of fact, the only thing he'd planned on holding was the remote for the television. He'd figured he deserved a couple of hours of downtime. It had been a long day.

A long week.

A long month.

A long year.

And now he was sitting in a hospital room, holding hands with a woman he'd been trying hard to avoid for the better part of two months.

He frowned, slipping his hand from hers.

Frowned again when she didn't move.

He touched the side of her neck the way he

had when he'd found her unconscious in her crumbled car, let his fingers linger on smooth skin and steady pulse.

"Don't worry. I haven't died, yet," she grumbled, and he let his hand drop away.

"Yet?"

"The way my head is pounding, I'm thinking my brain might explode." Her eyes opened slowly. Eyes the color of Loon Lake in early spring. Misty green-blue. He'd noticed them the day they'd met. Had told himself not to, but he'd been noticing them ever since, anyway.

"Let's hope it doesn't. Kane won't be happy if you die on my watch."

"I hope he won't be happy if I die, period." She flashed a smile that brought out the deep dimple in her cheek. Pretty. Wholesome. Not at all the way Jessica had been. No sultry allure or boldly painted lips. Rayne was all about subtle color and natural beauty.

"You remember Kane?"

"Sure. We spoke several times when I interviewed for my job with his company. I was really excited when he said he wanted to hire me. A new job. A new life," she mumbled, and he thought she might drift off again.

"Was that the plan?" In the seven weeks he'd known her, he hadn't asked why she'd moved from Arizona to Washington. Hadn't asked a hundred questions that he'd wanted to ask, because asking would have meant interest, and he couldn't allow himself to be interested again. To fall again.

Heart.

Soul.

Mind.

He'd done it once.

Had proven just how little he knew about what it meant to make it work. Failure hadn't been in his vocabulary, but he'd failed anyway. Hadn't given enough of himself, spent enough time, done enough to maintain what he'd been so eager to start.

"The plan? I don't know if I had one. I just wanted to get away from…"

"What?"

"Sometimes a person just needs a fresh start."

"I can understand that." He'd made his own fresh start two years ago. Come back to the place he'd grown up, tried to put the past and all its mistakes behind him.

"Yeah, well, it looks like I'm getting another

fresh start. Maybe you can fill me in on a few things." She rubbed the bridge of her nose, her face pale, the bump on her head deep blue and green.

"Like what?"

"When did we meet? How did I end up renting an apartment from your mother? Are we *just* coworkers or are we more?" she asked.

Straightforward.

Unapologetic.

Handling the situation in the same forthright manner she handled clients. He'd admired that, admired a lot of things about Rayne.

"We're coworkers. We attend the same church. Your apartment is in my mother's attic. Kane knew my mother was looking for a tenant, and he knew you were looking for a place to stay. He mentioned it to me." Chance had seen it as a win-win situation. His mother occupied with a renter who had a baby. Rayne provided with a comfortable home.

"So, we see each other outside of work sometimes?"

"Yes."

"That explains it, then."

"Explains what?"

"I can't remember anything after I left Phoenix, but your eyes are familiar." She blushed, pink coloring her pale cheeks.

"Like I said, we're not strangers, but we're not anything more than coworkers, either."

"Good."

"Good? I think I'm insulted," he said, and she smiled, flashing her dimple.

"It's nothing personal. I mean, if I were going to date again, I wouldn't discount you out of hand."

"That very…magnanimous of you."

"That's a big word, Chance, and my head is pounding too hard for a witty response. So how about I just say I'm out of the dating game and happy to be, and we leave it at that?"

"We can do that."

"Thanks." She closed her eyes, fell silent, and he let the conversation die.

She looked pale and fragile, her golden hair matted and stained with blood, but she was in better shape than her totaled car. It had flipped at least once when she ran off the road, and if she hadn't been wearing a seat belt, she'd probably be dead.

He frowned, pacing across the room and

staring out the window. Streetlights illuminated the parking lot, gleaming off the icy pavement. Not a good night for anyone to be out. Especially not someone who wasn't used to driving in slick conditions.

But Rayne had left a client and driven to the airport. Why? It was a question he wanted to ask. One he knew she couldn't answer. Below the window, someone moved through the parking lot, sticking to the shadows, avoiding the golden glow of the streetlights. Something about the figure's furtive movements made the hair on the back of Chance's neck stand on end.

As a chaplain in the army, he'd been in his share of danger zones. He knew the hair-raising, blood-pulsing feeling of impending trouble.

Someone was in my room.

That's what Rayne had said, and he'd chalked her fear up to head injury and confusion.

Maybe there was something more to it, though.

Something more than the cleaning crew or her imagination.

Footsteps sounded in the hall, and Chance tensed, turning as the door swung open.

A balding man in his mid-fifties stepped into the room. Lab coat buttoned, stethoscope hanging from his pocket, he pulled Rayne's chart from the end of the bed, glancing at it as he greeted Chance. "I'm Dr. Donahue. I'll be the attending physician while Ms. Sampson is here."

"That shouldn't be too long, Doctor. I'm planning on leaving as soon as you unhook me from this IV," Rayne said without opening her eyes.

"How about we see how you're doing before we talk about getting the IV out or going home?" The doctor flashed a light in Rayne's eyes, asked a few questions that she could answer, a few that she couldn't.

Chance should probably go.

Probably.

But he didn't.

Being a chaplain had hardwired him to be concerned for the sick and the struggling. Rayne was both.

That was a good enough reason to stay, but there were other reasons as well.

He might have spent the better part of two months avoiding her, but he hadn't been able to ignore Rayne. She'd made a good reputation for herself at work, a good reputation in the community. Chance's mother adored her. Everyone at Grace Christian Fellowship admired and respected her.

Chance would be lying if he said he hadn't been pulled in by her sweet smile and contagious energy. He might be out of the dating game, but he wasn't blind. So he was staying because he cared.

There was nothing wrong with that.

He could care without becoming too involved.

Sure you can.

He scowled, pacing back to the window as the doctor continued his examination. Outside, sheets of ice fell from the charcoal sky, pinging off the ground and cars, shimmering on trees and bushes. A shadow shifted at the edge of the lot, merged with another shadow. Two figures standing in the icy downpour at midnight with the wind chill dipping to twenty below?

Not something any sane person would do, but that didn't mean anything sinister was going on.

Someone was in my room.

Rayne's words drifted through his mind again, and he couldn't ignore them or the quicksilver shot of adrenaline that flooded his veins.

Maybe nothing was going on.

Probably nothing was.

But it wouldn't hurt to check things out.

He buttoned his coat, pulled on his gloves. "I'll be back in a minute."

"Where are you going?" Rayne asked, her eyes tracking his movements, her face pale as paper as the doctor probed the bump on her head.

"Just out to the parking lot."

"Why?"

Good question.

I'm going to chase shadows didn't seem like a good answer, so he kept it simple. "I need to check out a few things."

She frowned. "What things?"

"You ask an awful lot of questions for someone with a concussion. You know that?"

"You avoid a lot of questions for someone who has nothing to hide."

"Don't go anywhere while I'm gone, okay?" He walked into the corridor before she could respond, jogging down two flights of stairs and out into the frigid November night. Cold wind bit through his coat and whipped ice into his eyes, nearly blinding him.

Definitely *not* a night to stand in a parking lot chatting.

He pulled up his hood, used it to shield his eyes as he crossed the nearly empty lot. No sign of the men who'd been there. He stood where they'd been, looked at the building, his gaze drawn to the only lit room on the second floor.

Lights flashed at the far end of the lot, a car engine roaring to life. He watched as the truck crawled toward him. Tinted windows made it impossible to see the driver, but Chance's skin crawled, his body humming with adrenaline.

Danger.

He jumped back, nearly slipping on the ice.

The truck rolled by, turned onto the road, drove away.

Nothing unusual about someone leaving the hospital.

So why did Chance feel so uneasy?

He walked back into the hospital, jogged up the stairs, knocked on the door.

"Come in," Rayne called, and he stepped into the room, scowling when he caught sight of her. Somehow, in the few minutes he'd been gone, she'd managed to get rid of the doctor and pull on black slacks.

"What are you doing?"

"Trying to figure out how to get a shirtsleeve over this IV."

"I'm almost afraid to ask why."

"Then don't."

"You're ornery when you're hurt, Goldilocks."

"I'm ornery, period."

"So, why *are* you trying to get that sleeve over the IV?"

"I can't walk outside dressed in a hospital gown."

"You're planning to walk outside with an IV?"

"No. I'm planning to go down the hall and ask a nurse to remove the IV. Then I'm going to walk outside."

"And?"

"Hopefully, hitch a ride back to my apartment with you."

"What does the doctor think of that plan?"

"I didn't ask."

"But I'm sure he mentioned how long he thought you should stay."

"At least until tomorrow morning, but that's not working for me. I keep saying I need to be with my daughter, and I mean it." She shoved her feet into black pumps, clutching a sweater as if she really thought she was going to leave.

"You leaving isn't working for me."

"Then I guess we're at an impasse." She looked exhausted, the bruise on her head appearing deeper and more vivid. Another bruise stained her cheek, blue and black the only color on her pale face.

"You need to lie down. You're pale as paper."

"I need to see my daughter. I've tucked her into bed every night for eight months. She must have wondered where I was tonight. Wondered if I were coming back."

"My mother is taking good care of her."

"Your mother isn't *her* mother. I am. What if she wakes up tonight crying for me? And what about tomorrow morning when she wakes up and I'm not there?"

"She'll be—" He was going to say fine, but a tear slipped down Rayne's cheek.

She brushed it away impatiently, sniffed back more, and all his reasons for convincing her to stay at the hospital suddenly didn't seem nearly as important as getting her home to Emma.

"I'll get a nurse to take out the IV. You stay here."

"Thanks." She offered a watery smile, and something in his chest shifted, warmed. He ignored it.

It took a half hour to track down the doctor and find a nurse who wasn't too busy to unhook the IV.

Not a long time, but it seemed like an eternity, the clock ticking while Rayne sat alone in her hospital room.

Alone, and she'd seen someone standing in her room before Chance had found her crumbled on the ground.

Alone, and two men had been lingering in the hospital parking lot.

Alone.

Unprotected.

He jogged the last few yards to the room and walked in.

Rayne sat on the edge of the bed, a telephone pressed to her ear, a scowl etching lines in her pale face.

She met his eyes and frowned. "Didn't your mother ever teach you to knock?"

"The door was open. Why bother?"

"Because…" She paused, cocking her head to the side and speaking to whomever was on the other end of the phone line. "Yes, someone is here with me, and since you put me on hold… Look, Michael, *you* called *me*. I'm sorry the prayer chain gave you the impression that I was on death's door. I'm not. As a matter of fact, I feel fine."

"Liar," Chance mouthed, and Rayne wrinkled her nose and turned away.

"Thank you for your concern. Good night." She gently set the phone back in the receiver, and Chance had the distinct impression that she would rather have slammed it.

"I take it that wasn't a friend."

"My ex-fiancé. My mother called the prayer chain coordinator at my old church and told her I was awake and lucid. Michael just got home from work and got the message. He called to see how I was feeling."

"At one in the morning?"

"He said he didn't realize how late it was until he'd already dialed."

"Who doesn't know what time it is?"

"Michael. Were you able to find a nurse?" She changed the subject, and he went with it.

"Yes, I had to find the doctor and get him to write the order first. Sorry it took so long."

"Actually, I dozed off for a while and woke up when the phone rang, so it didn't seem like that long at all." She smoothed hair away from her bruised cheek, her hand trembling slightly.

From pain?

Fear?

Fatigue?

The phone call?

"Are you sure you're up to leaving?"

"I know I'm not up to staying." She stood and swayed, her eyes closing as she sagged toward him.

He grabbed her waist, his palms pressed against cool cotton and taut muscles.

"Sorry. I think I got up too quickly." She

eased away, and he had the urge to tighten his grip, hold on a little longer.

Not a good direction for his thoughts to be going.

"You'd better sit back down." His tone was gruffer than he'd intended, but Rayne didn't seem to notice.

She also didn't seem to have noticed that he'd told her to sit down.

She crossed the room, and dug through the bag of things his mother had packed and brought to the hospital earlier. He hadn't looked inside but, knowing his mother, it contained everything Rayne would need for a month-long stay.

"Did you pack all this?" Rayne asked, pulling out a blue shirt, her hands still shaking.

She definitely needed to sit down.

"My mother did. Now how about you do what I suggested and sit before you fall?"

"I'm not going to fall." But she sat anyway, dropping into a chair so quickly he wondered if her legs had gone out from under her.

He grabbed a pitcher of water from the table near the bed and poured some into a paper cup. "Here, drink this."

"I'd rather not."

"And I'd rather not watch you pass out."

"Would you rather watch me lose my lunch?"

"That bad, huh?" He grabbed a paper towel from the bathroom, wetted it and pressed it against the back of her neck. Silky curls fell across his knuckles, and he caught the muted scent of flowers and rain drifting from her hair. A breath of spring amid the antiseptic smells that lingered in the hospital.

"I'll be okay. I just need some fresh air."

If her pallor was any indication, she needed more than fresh air, but before Chance could say as much, a nurse bustled into the room, eyeing Rayne with the same concern Chance felt.

"I hear you've decided to leave us," the nurse said, and Rayne nodded.

"I have to get home to my daughter."

"How will you care for your daughter if you can't care for yourself?"

"I'll—"

"My mother will help out," Chance cut in. Arguing wasn't going to do any of them any good. Rayne had made up her mind. The best thing they could do was move things along so he could get her home where she could rest—and where he could keep her safe.

The nurse took out the IV, and Chance walked out into the hall, waiting there while Rayne changed.

Definitely a long day working its way into a long night, and he wasn't even sure why he was at the hospital waiting for Rayne. She'd made plenty of friends since she'd moved to Spokane. He could have called any one of them.

He hadn't.

"All right. We're ready." The nurse wheeled Rayne into the hall, and Chance followed them down to the lobby and out into the early-morning darkness. Beyond the portico, the pavement glistened with ice, the winter storm still howling.

Why *had* Rayne left a meeting with a client and driven to the airport on such a terrible night?

He drove his SUV to the portico, helped Rayne into the passenger seat.

"We have a twenty-minute ride ahead of us. Why don't you rest for a while?"

She didn't respond, just leaned her head back

and closed her eyes, the bruises on her face dark and angry-looking.

He pulled out onto the highway, ice turning to snow as he crawled along the slick road and into the hills of Green Bluff. Within minutes, white powder covered the road and the thick evergreens that lined it. The world lay silent and still, everyone and everything taking cover from the weather.

The dirt road that led to the farm and orchards where he'd grown up curved around barren fields. He passed the cottage he'd been living in since he'd left the army. Passed the matching cottage that his mother's only farmhand used.

The farmhouse stood a quarter mile away, the porch light burning brightly the same way it had every night of Chance's childhood.

Home.

That's what it felt like. As a kid, he'd dreamed of big cities and exciting people. He'd wanted the thrill that came with new places and new faces. Working as an army chaplain had given him an opportunity to experience those things. For ten years, he'd served God, served his country, served his own desire to explore the world.

Now…

What?

He was backtracking, finding the easy pace of small-town life more fulfilling than he'd imagined it could be. Finding that serving God could be done just as easily at home as it could far away and finding it way too easy to forget the mistakes of the past and embrace something new.

He frowned, glancing at Rayne as he pulled into his mother's driveway.

He wasn't *embracing* anything. He was helping out a coworker, bringing a young mother home safe to her daughter, doing the kind of thing he'd done dozens of times over the years.

He was helping. Then he was going home and getting a few hours of sleep before the sun came up and another day began. He had a client to meet with in the morning. A fence to fix at the edge of the orchards. A to-do list half a mile long.

Rayne was just one more thing on that list.

Get her home safe.

That's all he'd needed to do.

He'd done it.

Mission accomplished.

Somehow, though, as he opened the door and rounded the SUV, he had a feeling there was going to be a whole lot more to *keeping* Rayne safe than simply getting her home.

THREE

"Rayne?" Someone nudged her shoulder, and Rayne pushed the hand away, wanting to sink back into dreams and away from the throbbing pain in her head.

"Go away." She didn't open her eyes. No sense doing that, seeing as how she had no intention of moving. Every breath, every heartbeat brought more pain, and she had no desire to see what would happen if she actually did more.

"Come on, Goldilocks, are you really going to make me carry you?" The words were muttered against her ear as she was scooped up, pressed close to a hard chest.

Goldilocks?

Not Michael, then. He only ever called her *Rayne*. No *sweetie* or *darling* or *honey*. Just *Rayne*.

"I can walk," she mumbled, but she didn't want to walk, didn't want to even open her eyes.

"Sure you can." Not a stranger's voice, and she tried to grasp a memory, hold on to it long enough to remember where she'd heard it.

Cold wind stung her cheeks, and she shivered as the world shifted and moved beneath her. A door opened, warmth replaced cold, and she knew she should open her eyes, look around, see where she was. Instead, she let her head rest against solid warmth, let herself drift away again.

"Chance! You scared twenty years off my life!" A female voice pulled her from darkness, and she opened her eyes, saw nothing but thick black leather. A coat. Chance's coat. Images flashed through her mind. Blue-gray eyes and a hard, handsome face. New memories, not the missing ones, but at least she had them.

She just needed to turn her head, and she'd see the woman who'd spoken, but Rayne wasn't sure moving was a good idea. Her stomach churned, bile rising up as Chance shifted his grip.

"Sorry, Mom. Rayne insisted on leaving the hospital and coming back to take care of Emma."

"She's a good mother. I wouldn't have expected anything less. How is she doing?"

"Probably about as good as she looks."

About as good as she looked?

She must look horrible.

"Just so you know, I'm awake, and I can hear every word you're saying. If you plan on going into excruciating details about how terrible I look, I'd rather you not." She managed to lift her head, and met the eyes of a sixty-something woman with salt-and-pepper curls and a barely lined face.

"You're beautiful, bruises and all, my dear. Put her on the couch, Chance. It's warmer than the back bedroom."

"You mean the room I spent eighteen years of my life in?"

"Your father and I offered to let you sleep upstairs when you were five, but you were afraid the bogeyman would get you."

"Yeah, and by the time I was a teenager, I liked the idea of ground-floor windows."

"If we'd known that, we'd probably have insisted that you take one of the rooms in the upstairs apartment."

"That's exactly why you didn't know." Chance carried Rayne into a dark living room and set her on a couch that faced an oversize stone fireplace.

"Thanks. Next time, I'll carry you," she said, and he smiled, his face softening, his eyes warm in the darkness.

"I'm not sure we'd both survive that. You're kind of puny."

"Puny? I'm strong as an ox."

"But much prettier," he said, and then frowned, backing away, letting his mother move in to cover Rayne with a blanket.

"How are you feeling, dear?"

"I'm okay."

"Thank the Lord. I was worried sick when you didn't come home after work. You've never been late before."

"I'm sorry I worried you."

"Please, don't apologize. I'm just glad I knew enough to be worried. Another couple of hours in that ditch, and you could have frozen to… Well, it doesn't bear thinking about. You're going to be okay, and that's all that matters." She patted Rayne's hand, the motherly gesture reminding Rayne of all the things she'd left behind in Arizona.

"In case you're wondering, Rayne, this is my mother, Lila Richardson."

"You're introducing me as if I haven't been her landlord for a couple of months." Lila laughed, apparently not realizing how serious the situation was.

Nearly two months in Washington.

Not even one memory.

"She has partial amnesia, Mom. She doesn't remember anything after she left Arizona."

Lila's amusement slipped away, and she patted Rayne's hand again. "I'm so sorry, Rayne. I didn't mean to make light of things. Tell you what, I'll bring you some tea. That should help you relax and sleep."

"I'd like to see Emma first." She sat up, ignoring the pain and dizziness that followed. She couldn't sleep, wouldn't sleep until she saw Emma, made sure she was okay. No matter how well she might have known Lila before the accident, Rayne knew nothing about her now. The nurse's words had been comforting, but something niggled at Rayne's mind every time she thought of her daughter. Fear. She knew the feeling, had felt it the day she'd had a gun pointed at her head, but she shouldn't be feeling it now, sitting in a cozy living room.

She needed to see Emma.

Needed to hold her.

Need to make sure that her fears were unfounded, that her daughter really was safe.

"She's in the guest room. Chance, why don't you bring her out here? That way Rayne won't have to get up."

"I'm not sure waking a baby up at two in the morning is a good idea," Chance said, not moving.

He was right, of course.

It didn't make sense to pull Emma out of bed, but Rayne *was* going to see her. She stood, all the blood draining from her head.

"Careful." Chance eased her back down onto the sofa, and she knew she wasn't going anywhere.

"It won't hurt Emma to see her mommy, and I know you'll sleep better once *you've* seen *her*,"

Lila said. "Don't put anymore mother guilt on her, Chance. She's been through enough without adding that into the mix. You go get the baby while I make the tea. Rayne, you just stay right where you are and let us take care of you."

Let them take care of her?

Wasn't that breaking rule number one?

Rayne was certain it was, but she did exactly what Lila said.

Sat.

Right there on the couch. Waiting for other people to take care of her and her daughter.

Mother guilt?

Yeah. She knew all about that. Had felt it almost every day since Chandra died and she'd become Emma's legal guardian.

Guilt because she had to work.

Guilt because she didn't spend every minute of every day caring for her daughter.

Guilt because she hadn't been there to see Emma roll over for the first time, crawl for the first time.

You're not ready to be a mother, Rayne.

In some ways, Michael had been right, but Rayne wasn't sure any woman was ever truly prepared for motherhood. She just had to work hard to be the best mother she could be. That would be enough.

She hoped.

"Do you want me to get her, Rayne?" Chance asked.

Such an easy question to answer, but Rayne's brain seemed to be misfiring, her thoughts scattered. "I don't know."

"Then I'll get her." He walked across the room and down a narrow hallway, and she waited, afraid to move for fear the room would move with her.

Seconds later, Chance reappeared, Emma resting against his shoulder. Bright red hair. Big blue eyes, slowly blinking open. Chubby cheeks. She had little of Chandra's dark exotic beauty, though the almond shape of her eyes and the fullness of her lips reminded Rayne of her childhood friend.

"There she is, kid. Mommy is home." Chance shifted Emma so she could see Rayne, and the baby reached out, babbling excitedly.

"Mamamamamama."

Chance set her on Rayne's lap, and the scent of baby lotion and formula filled Rayne's nose.

It was the best kind of perfume. The most wonderful aroma.

She smiled, kissing Emma's soft curls, and hugging her close. "I missed you, baby."

Missed an entire two months of her life.

"I see the princess is awake and raring to go." Lila walked back into the room, carrying a tray that contained a mug and a plate of cookies and setting it on the coffee table.

"Hopefully, she won't stay awake when Rayne is ready to sleep."

Ready?

She'd passed ready. Her eyes drooped, her arms felt heavy, and it was all she could do to hold Emma. Pain throbbed behind her eyes, speared through her skull, but she didn't want to give in to it. Didn't want to put Emma down or hand her to someone else.

Eight months ago, she'd agreed to be guardian to Chandra's baby if anything were to happen to Chandra. She hadn't thought it through when she'd agreed, hadn't taken more than five minutes to consider how becoming a mother would change her life, hadn't prayed about it, hadn't done any of the things she usually did when faced with major decisions.

Probably because there really hadn't been any decision to make. She and Chandra had been best friends since kindergarten, and there was nothing Rayne would have refused her. And even though the decision had been hasty, Rayne couldn't regret it. Emma was the best thing in her life.

"Mamamamam." Emma grabbed a fistful of Rayne's hair, holding it tight in her chubby hand as she bounced with excitement.

"Careful, kid. Your mom already has a headache. She doesn't need you adding to it." Chance unraveled hair from Emma's fist, smiling as the baby grabbed his nose.

"Why don't I take her back into the room, get her settled back down before she's too wide-awake?" Lila reached for Emma, and Rayne didn't have the strength to protest. She loved her daughter, wanted to care for her, but her leaden body refused to do anything but sag into the couch.

"Thank you, Mrs. Richardson."

"No need to thank me. I love having a baby around the house. And you've always called me Lila. There's no need to change that now."

Lila smiled as she carried Emma back down the hall.

"Your mother seems like a wonderful lady."

"She thinks you are, too." Chance grabbed a cookie and bit into it, holding the plate out to Rayne.

Her stomach lurched and she shook her head. Regretted it immediately when the lurching sensation grew worse. She felt dizzy and sick, her thoughts sliding away.

"Take a deep breath, Rayne. You've gone ten shades of pale." Chance pressed his hand to her forehead, the warm, dry feel of his palm anchoring her to the moment.

"I'll be okay."

"You've said that several times tonight, but you haven't convinced me yet." He handed her the mug, and she took a small sip of the flowery brew, her hand shaking, tea sloshing over her wrist.

"Careful." Chance wiped the liquid up with a napkin, and Rayne set the mug down on a coaster, not sure she trusted herself to keep holding it.

Done in.

That's how she felt.

All she wanted to do was lie back, close her eyes and try to forget the pounding pain.

"I think it's time to say goodnight," Chance said, and Rayne realized she'd closed her eyes, was slumping forward.

If she slumped any farther, she'd be face-down on the floor.

She straightened, nodded. "You're right. Sleep is about all I seem capable of."

"I'll head out then. If you're up to it, I'll stop by tomorrow. I have a few questions I'd like to ask when you're feeling better."

"Questions about what?"

"The accident."

"I don't remember it, so any questions will be impossible to answer."

"I know, but you were working with one of my clients last night. You'd told my mother you'd be back by five. When you didn't show, she called me, and I called the client who said you'd asked for directions to the airport before you'd left."

"I did?" She couldn't remember, and trying to push through the fog, grab the memories and hold on to them made her feel sick and disoriented.

"That's how I was able to find you. I retraced the route to the airport and spotted your car in the ravine. Do you have any idea if you were expecting a friend or family member to fly in?"

"I…really don't know." It was possible, though. She couldn't remember anything after leaving Arizona, but she remembered everything prior to that. Remembered all her friends who'd promised to come for a visit.

Maybe one of them had.

Thoughts swirled and whirled, images flying through her brain too quickly to grasp.

Darkness.

Bright light.

Fear.

The accident?

"It's possible, but if I'd picked someone up at the airport, wouldn't he or she have been with me in the car?"

"Maybe you didn't make it to the airport. The police think you lost control going around a curve in the road. The pavement was covered with a sheet of ice, so it's impossible to know which direction you were heading."

"Then whoever was waiting would have called to find out why I wasn't there, right?"

"For someone with a concussion, you're thinking fast. Want to check your cell phone?" He smiled, handing her a familiar black purse.

Finally, something she remembered.

Of course, she'd had it for a couple of years, so that wasn't such good news after all.

She pulled out her cell phone, scrolled through her call history. "The last call came in at five last evening. It's not a number I know."

"That would have been a few minutes before your meeting. How about we call and see who it is?"

"Okay." But concentrating on the numbers made her head spin, and she handed him the phone and leaned back against the couch cushions.

"You're done in. Tomorrow will be soon enough. I'm going to write down the number, though. I have a friend in the police department who might be able to trace it for us. I'll give him a call and see what he can come up with."

"It would be a lot easier if I could just remember."

"Memories or not, we'll figure out what happened."

"We?" She looked into his eyes, felt a quicksilver moment of awareness, knew that she'd looked into his eyes before, been drawn into his gaze.

"Why not?"

Because she had a feeling spending time with Chance could be dangerous. Because she could get lost looking into his eyes and forget all the reasons why relationships weren't for her. Because she had three rules—three perfectly good rules—for heart-healthy living, and there was no way she planned to break any of them.

"I…don't know."

"Then how about we just go with it for now?" He patted her knee, the warmth of his palm seeping through her slacks and into her chilled flesh.

The rules, Rayne. Don't forget about the rules.

But they were hard to remember with her head pounding and her stomach churning. Hard to remember when she was looking into Chance's eyes, feeling the warmth of his touch. She wanted to lean on him. She really did. And that terrified her.

"Since I'm too tired to argue, I guess we

will." She tried to smile, knew it fell flat. She needed him to leave before she threw herself into his arms and begged for him to stay.

"Are you sure you're going to be okay?" Chance asked, and she nodded, because she had no choice. Emma depended on her.

A welcome responsibility, even if it was a heavy one.

A responsibility Michael hadn't wanted.

His response to Emma had taught Rayne just how careful she needed to be with her heart. Not just because she didn't want it broken again, but because she couldn't risk Emma attaching to a man who would turn his back and walk away when things got tough.

Rayne closed her eyes, wishing she could block out pain and worry as easily as she could block out the sight of Chance.

"Good night." Fingers brushed her cheek, there and gone so quickly she wondered if she'd imagined them. A door opened, cold air whipping into the room before it clicked shut again.

And then she was alone.

Just Rayne and her thoughts.

Fun.

She shifted so she was lying down, her head

on a throw pillow, the blanket clutched around her shoulders.

She'd wanted her new life to be fun, exciting and filled with adventure, but a car accident, a concussion and amnesia were more of an adventure than she'd bargained for.

"You could cut me a break, Lord," she whispered, then became aware of the muted sound of a woman singing drifting into the room.

Lila singing Emma to sleep?

It had to be.

The knowledge warmed her.

Perhaps her prayer had been answered before she'd even uttered it.

Rayne had fallen far before she'd moved to Spokane, her once-charmed life crumbling around her. But as she listened to Lila's quiet singing, felt the comforting warmth of the old farmhouse settling around her, she couldn't help thinking that in the midst of all the falling, God had found her a very soft place to land.

FOUR

Coffee.

About a gallon should do it.

Chance reached for the pot, filled a mug and sipped the hot brew. It used to be he could pull an all-nighter and feel just fine. Not anymore. Now he needed sleep about as much as he needed food and air.

He scowled, topping off his coffee and grabbing his coat from the back of the kitchen chair. He had a meeting with a client at nine, and he needed to check in with his mother before then.

Check in with *Rayne* before then.

He couldn't get the image of two men standing in an ice storm out of his head.

Couldn't shake the words that kept echoing through his mind.

Someone was in my room.

He'd called the hospital, spoken to security personnel and gotten the head security officer to look through surveillance tapes. He'd confirmed what Rayne had claimed. A man had stood in the doorway of her room for several seconds, then hurried away as late-night visitors walked into the hallway.

The knowledge had fueled Chance's search, and he'd called the number from Rayne's phone—hadn't been surprised when no one answered.

He didn't like loose ends, and that's all a night of searching had uncovered.

Loose end after loose end after loose end.

Which didn't sit well.

As a matter of fact, it made him downright irritable.

Not the best way to begin the day, but since he hadn't ever really ended the previous night, Chance wouldn't hold it against himself.

He grabbed a granola bar from the cupboard, took another quick sip of coffee and walked outside. A thick layer of snow blanketed the ground and clung to barren apple trees. In the distance, a plow moved slowly along the main road, and gray smoke drifted from the chimney of Old Man Jefferson's house.

Every part of the landscape, every bite of cold wind, every waft of burning wood whispered home, and Chance relaxed for the first time in hours. He hadn't planned to ever return to Washington to live. He'd left for college at eighteen, gotten a degree in theology and joined the army as a chaplain. He'd traveled the world, visited big cities and rural towns.

He'd met Jessica.

Married.

Separated.

Become a widower.

Never once had he thought about returning to Green Bluff and the family orchards.

Strange how the thing he'd least thought he wanted was exactly what he seemed to need.

Or maybe not so strange.

God had a way of moving His people in the direction in which He wanted them to go.

No matter how much they protested.

The porch light still shone as he pulled into his mother's driveway, and Chance frowned as he eyed the house's dark facade. It had been a late night. More than likely, everyone was just sleeping late, but it wasn't like his mother to keep the light burning past dawn.

He jogged up the porch steps, bracing himself as he stepped into the dark foyer.

Silence.

His pulse jumped, and he veered into the living room, stopping short when he saw Rayne.

Dressed in well-worn jeans and a fluffy-looking blue sweater, she sat in the old rocking chair, Emma lying against her shoulder, both of them relaxed and content.

And beautiful.

Something unfurled in his chest, warmth moving in and setting up camp.

Warmth toward Rayne.

Toward Emma.

Toward the picture they made sitting in his grandmother's rocking chair.

This was what he'd once imagined coming home to—the stunning beauty of a mother nurturing her child. In those heady days after he'd married Jessica, he'd thought of building a family, believed that he'd walk in on scenes like this one over and over again.

It had never happened, of course. Jessica hadn't wanted anything to distract from their love. That's what she'd said.

But in Chance's mind, the more love was given, the more it grew.

"Is she sleeping?" he asked, and Rayne nodded.

"Finally. She's been awake and grumpy since four."

"Then you didn't get much rest." He settled onto the couch. No blankets there. No pillow. No indication that Rayne had ever slept.

"Neither did your mother. I feel terrible for causing so much trouble."

"I'm sure my mother doesn't think it was trouble. Is she around?" The unease he'd felt when he'd pulled into the driveway was still there, nipping at his heels.

"She's out getting wood for the fireplace. I offered to help, but she called me an invalid and told me not to move a muscle while she was gone."

"How long has she been out there?"

"A few minutes."

A few minutes to grab a couple of pieces of wood from the back deck?

"I'll give her a hand." He hurried through the house, stepped out onto the deck, his heart lurching when he realized his mother wasn't there.

Had she gone for a walk?

Run into trouble?

He'd lost his father and brother in a car accident two years ago. He didn't want to lose his mother, too.

Footprints led him across the yard and past the old barn. His mother stood a hundred feet away, leaning on the gate that separated their property from the forested hills beyond and talking to her farmhand, Fred Jagusch.

"Isn't it a little cold to be outside today?" Chance called, and both turned to face him.

"I could say the same to you, Chance. What are you doing here so early?" His mother hurried over, her cheeks pink with cold.

"It's almost eight."

"Maybe it just feels early because of all the chaos last night." Fred walked over. A fixture on the farm for as long as Chance could remember, he helped during apple-picking season and did odd jobs the rest of the year in exchange for room and board.

"Speaking of chaos, I need to get back to the house to pull the biscuits from the oven before they burn. Come in when you're done, Fred, and have some breakfast."

"Now, Ms. Lila, you know how I feel about imposing."

"How is it imposing to accept a meal from a friend?" Chance's mother threw the question over her shoulder as she hurried away.

"That woman sure has a way of bossing people around," Fred grumbled, but Chance knew he'd take the food as he had every weekday morning for the past few decades.

"She's got a way of feeding people she cares about."

"That, too. Saw her out getting wood when I came to look at the back gate. Next thing I know, she's trying to help me."

"Is something wrong with the gate?"

"Nope, but someone drove past my house last night. Took him a long time to realize that this road dead-ends at the farmhouse."

"How long?"

"Good thirty minutes. I just figured your

mom was having visitors until she called from the hospital and said Rayne had been in an accident. Figured maybe kids cut the lock on the gate and went snowmobiling through the woods, but the gate is just fine."

"What time did the car drive by?"

"Must have been around nine. Your mother called me close to ten."

"Strange time for someone to be driving unfamiliar country roads," Chance said, more to himself than to Fred.

"That's why I thought it was kids. What kind of moron drives dark, windy roads in the middle of an ice storm?"

Maybe the same kind of person who snuck into an unconscious woman's hospital room and stood watching her.

Chance didn't like the direction his thoughts were taking, but he couldn't find another path for them to go.

Something was going on.

Something more than an accident.

If he wanted to keep Rayne and Emma safe, he had to find out what.

"Did you get a look at the car?"

"What? You think my life is so dull, I look at every car that drives by my place?"

"It was a simple question, Fred."

"And I'll give you a simple answer. My life *is* that dull, and I did see the truck. Dark and foreign. Newish-looking."

"Should I ask if you got a plate number?"

"Should have, but didn't. There a reason why you want it?"

"Just a feeling I have." *A bad one.*

"Always go with your gut. That's my motto. I'll keep my eyes and ears open. If I see it again, I'll let you know."

"Thanks. I need to get going. I've got a meeting this morning."

"More of that private eye stuff?"

"It's not stuff. It's a job."

"There are plenty of jobs to do around here, son. No need to go looking for more."

"It takes money to do the kind of jobs this place needs. No job, no money."

"Guess you've got a point. Just be careful. Your ma already lost her husband and one boy. She don't need to lose another."

Fred's parting shot followed Chance as he

walked through the mudroom and into his mother's kitchen.

Bacon.

Biscuits.

Eggs.

He recognized the scents but didn't see the food, couldn't seem to see anything but Rayne. Blond curls springing around her face, deep bruises on her forehead and cheek. Pale skin. Pale pink lips. She looked exhausted.

She also looked good.

Worse than good, she looked like she fit.

Right there in the same chair Jessica had sat in when she'd come to meet the family. Only Jessica had looked too polished, too perfect, her exotic appearance overshadowing the room's old-time charm. Rayne's beauty added to the charm, warmed the room, made it seem even more like home.

"Hi. Again." Rayne's gaze skittered away as if she sensed his thoughts.

"Is Emma in bed?"

"In bed and sleeping soundly," his mother responded, setting a plate of food in front of Rayne, and then shoving one into Chance's hands.

"I don't have time to eat, Mom."

"You will if you stop talking and chew."

Rayne laughed, the soft sound drawing Chance's attention back to her pink lips, her smooth skin, her misty-blue eyes.

"You're laughing, but *you* haven't started chewing yet, either." Lila placed a glass of orange juice in front of Rayne, and Chance remembered her doing the same for him hundreds of times ever since he was a kid. No matter how old he'd gotten, no matter that teenage years had turned him truculent, the breakfast routine had never grown old.

"Are you always so tough, Lila?" Rayne asked. Then she must have realized it was something she should have known. Her amusement faded, and she pushed a piece of bacon around her plate with a fork, lost in thoughts she didn't share.

"Only with people I care about." As always, Lila took things in stride, pouring coffee into three mugs, dumping three sugars into one and handing it to Rayne.

"It's nice and sweet, dear. Take a sip. Maybe it will put some color in your cheeks. I'm going to start a fire in the living room. The wind is howling today, and this house isn't well-insulated."

"Let me take care of that, Mom." Chance set his half-empty plate on the counter, but his mother was already at the threshold of the kitchen.

"I can manage."

And then she was gone, humming under her breath as she moved through the house, humming because she was finally getting what she'd been wanting.

Chance and Rayne alone.

"Your mother was right. The coffee is helping," Rayne said, as she set the mug on the table, ran her thumb over the rim. Refused to look him in the eye.

"My mother is right about most things." Though she was wrong if she thought that Chance and Rayne would end up together.

"I haven't known many men who would say that."

"Then maybe you haven't known many of the right men."

"No?" She finally looked him in the eye, her half smile just enough to showcase the dimple in her cheek.

"Real men appreciate their mothers' wisdom."

"Is that your two cents for the day?" she asked, her smile broadening.

"For the week."

"I wish you'd given it to me three years ago. I could have avoided…" Her voice trailed off, and she shook her head. "Never mind."

"Let me guess." He dropped into the chair across from her. "Your ex called his mother five times a day and lived in her basement but had absolutely no respect for her opinion?"

Her eyes widened for a moment, and then she laughed. "Hardly. Michael had a gorgeous house in the Phoenix suburbs, and he lived by himself. But he thought he was smarter than his mother. Based on your two cents, that should have been a clue that something wasn't right."

"Sounds like Michael is a fool."

"Michael is very smart, very accomplished and very charming."

"Yet he's in Phoenix, and you're here. As I said, he's a fool."

"I'm sure if he were here, that would be up for debate." She crossed the room, dumped the contents of her plate into the slop bucket near the mudroom door. Did she remember doing it before or was she simply mimicking what his mother did every morning?

"Looks like you're familiar with the slop bucket."

"The one that your mom feeds the pig from? She told me all about it this morning. I think she was afraid I'd be embarrassed about all the things I can't remember, so she tried to point out some things I should know."

"So no memories of your life here?"

"None."

"And none of the accident?"

"That would make life easier, wouldn't it? I could explain things to my insurance adjuster and to the police and to everyone else who asks what happened. Unfortunately, it's not the way things are. I can't remember anything. The more I try, the emptier the void seems to be."

"So don't try. It'll come back to you. One way or another."

"That's what the doctor said, but…"

"What?"

"I checked my answering machine in the apartment this morning. No one called here last night. No message from a friend waiting for me at the airport. I tried to check emails, but everything was gone. No emails before this morning."

"Is that typical?"

"I clean out my email files about as often as I clean out my purse."

"Which means?"

"Not often enough. Every few months, I get sick of the mess and go to work. I guess yesterday was my day to clean out my inbox." She shrugged, her face tight with frustration, exhaustion and pain.

"You checked for deleted files?"

"I checked everything and found nothing. Two months of my life is completely gone. I can't find one clue as to what I was doing, where I was going, who I was communicating with."

"There may be a way to retrieve the files. Want me to look into it?"

"Will it make any difference? I went to the airport for some reason. I got into an accident I don't remember. I'm alive. I'll be fine. That's all that matters, right?" She leaned her hip against the counter and smoothed her hair, her sweater riding up just enough to reveal a sliver of skin.

Soft.

That's how she looked. Soft sweater. Soft jeans. Soft eyes.

But she wasn't soft.

She'd moved away from everything she'd known, started a new job in a new town without any help from friends or family, and she'd done it all with a baby in tow.

In Chance's estimation, that made her pretty tough.

Tough enough to handle what he was about to say.

"There *was* someone in your hospital room last night, Rayne." He laid it out. Plain and simple. No sense in doing anything else.

"I was hoping it was just a dream."

"Do you remember what he looked like?"

"Medium height. Thin. I couldn't see his face, but…"

"What?"

"It sounds crazy."

"Say it anyway."

"Just looking at him scared me." She shivered, her face a shade paler than it had been.

"Do you have a reason to believe someone would want to hurt you?"

"Not that I can remember."

"No enemies back in Arizona?"

"There was an incident a couple of months ago."

"Incident?"

"I worked at a shelter for abused women. The husband of one of the residents threatened me."

"A verbal threat?"

"He had a gun. I found out later that it wasn't loaded. At the time, though, I really thought I was going to die. That's one of the reasons I moved to Spokane. I wanted a fresh start and a job that didn't put me in that kind of danger."

It's what she'd wanted, but was it what she'd gotten?

Trouble had a way of following people, and it was possible the gunman had followed Rayne.

Stood in the doorway of her hospital room.

Meant to finish what he'd begun in Arizona?

He didn't know, but Chance planned to find out.

"Did the gunman go to prison?" If so, he'd call the Phoenix P.D. and see if he was still there.

"Since the gun wasn't loaded, the judge gave him probation."

"So he might have followed you here?"

"If he did, he'll go to prison for violating the terms of his probation."

Good.

Except that sending the guy to jail for violating probation wouldn't do Rayne a whole lot of good if she were dead.

FIVE

Someone *had* been in her hospital room.

The thought filled Rayne with cold dread, and she grabbed her coffee, sipping the warm, sweet liquid. It did nothing to ease the chill.

"I have a meeting this morning, but if you give me the guy's name, I'll check with Phoenix P.D., see if he's still in town. Once we know that, we'll know a little more about what we're dealing with. Or what we're *not* dealing with."

We.

He'd said that before.

She hadn't liked it then.

She liked it even less now.

Because she wasn't sure she could say no to the partnership. Wasn't sure she could turn her back on his help. She felt weak, shaky and unsure. Tired beyond anything she'd ever experienced.

Relying on Chance was a dangerous temptation, but if she gave in to it, there might not be any way to go back.

"I can call them myself."

"Before or after you collapse into bed and sleep for a week?" he asked, his light eyes staring straight into hers, daring her to deny that sleeping had been her plan.

"It shouldn't take me more than a few minutes to find out what we need to know."

"It shouldn't, but it might. Let me take care of this for you, okay? And if I ever have a concussion and need to call the police department, you can take care of it for me." He brushed strands of hair from her shoulder, his hand resting there, and she thought that if she listened to his voice, looked into his eyes for even a second longer, she might agree to anything he had to say.

So stop looking into his eyes and say *something!*

"His name is Darren Leon."

Say something. *Not* that.

He smiled, his hand dropping away. "I'll be back around noon."

He walked out of the kitchen, and Rayne could breathe again.

Breathe.

Think.

Wonder what had possessed her to agree to his plan.

No more relying on other people.

That was rule number one for heart-healthy living.

Rule number one.

Broken.

She rinsed out her coffee cup, her legs unsteady, her hands shaking. She blamed both on the concussion, but that was only part of the problem.

Something about Chance unbalanced her.

Had she felt that way the day they'd met? Felt that way during the time they'd known each other?

Or was her reaction some strange side effect of her head injury?

Either way, she needed to get over it, because she could *not* break rule number two. If she did, rule number three wouldn't be far behind.

And if she broke that one…

It didn't bear thinking about.

Not when she had so many more pressing things to worry about.

Someone had been in her hospital room.

She shuddered, hurried out of the kitchen and back into the living room. Empty. No sign of Chance or his mother, but a fire burned in the fireplace, the flames crackling and warm. She wanted to sink down in front of it, rest her eyes for a while, but she needed to check on Emma. Normally cheerful and happy, the baby had fussed from the time she'd awakened at four until she'd fallen asleep several hours later. She hadn't been feverish, but Rayne couldn't help worrying.

She walked down the hall and into the guest room. Set up as a nursery, it sported a cherrywood crib with soft blue bedding, a rocking chair and a changing table.

Emma lay sleeping in the middle of the crib, her cheeks pink, her hair curling. Rayne touched the baby's forehead, relieved to feel cool, dry skin.

Still no fever.

Maybe Emma simply needed more sleep.

Rayne knew *she* did.

"Is she still sleeping?" Lila whispered as she stepped into the room.

"Like a log."

"Why don't you go lie down for a while, too? I have some cross-stitching to do, and I'll just sit here and keep an eye on Emma while I do it."

"Cross-stitching?" It didn't seem like Lila's style. Spunky and energetic, Rayne's landlord seemed more like the kind to chop wood than stitch wall hangings.

"A gift for a friend who had hip replacement surgery." Lila settled into the rocking chair and pulled out the project.

"How's she doing?"

"Great. The surgery was five years ago, and she hasn't had a problem with that hip since. The quilt I bought and gave her while she was recovering is hanging on the wall in her living room. *This*—" she held up the cross-stitch pattern "—sits beside my bed and reminds me to never, ever try to cross-stitch a gift for a friend again."

Rayne laughed, cutting the sound short when Emma whimpered.

The baby settled down immediately, falling back into deep sleep.

"You'd better lie down while you still can. Chance will be back at noon, and I thought we'd try to get you to the doctor sometime after that."

"I'd rather just spend the day sleeping."

"That's exactly why you need to go to the doctor," Lila said in a tone that brooked no argument.

That was fine.

Rayne was too exhausted to argue.

Too tired to do more than walk into the living room, lie down on the couch and pull a blanket over herself.

Silence.

Warmth.

She couldn't keep her eyes open. Didn't even try. Just let herself slip into darkness and dreams.

He'd followed her.

She knew he had, and she clutched the steering wheel with both hands, her heart pounding with frustration and anger.

No more discussion.

No more talks.

He had to be held accountable for what he'd done.

Headlights illuminated the interior of the car, splashed across the pavement.

His headlights?

Coming fast. Too fast for the conditions. Passing her. Disappearing around a curve in the road.

Gone?

She rounded the curve. Saw the car too late.

She jerked the wheel, felt the tires slide on ice. Felt terror and grief for what she would lose if she died.

And then, nothing.

"Rayne?" Someone touched her shoulder, and she came up swinging, her fist just missing a hard, stubble-covered jaw.

Stubble?

Jaw?

She blinked, saw a familiar face. Familiar eyes.

"Chance?"

"Who were you expecting?"

Who had she been expecting?

The man who'd chased her in her dreams. She just shrugged. "I don't know. What time is it?"

"Nearly twelve-thirty."

Twelve-thirty?

She'd slept for over three hours?

"I need to check on Emma." She jumped to her feet, and the world spun.

"Not so fast, Rayne. Your ending up on the floor won't do Emma any good." Chance's hands gripped her waist, his fingers warm through her sweater. She wanted to lean her head against his chest, close her eyes and block out the spinning motion.

Wanted to.

Didn't dare.

Rule number two: no men. Ever. No matter what.

"I'm okay." She backed away, trying hard not to look into his eyes.

That's where she'd gone wrong with Michael. She'd looked into his eyes, imagined all kinds of things that weren't really there and fallen straight into dreams of happily-ever-after.

"So is Emma. My mom is feeding her a bottle, and *we* need to get going. You have a doctor's appointment in an hour."

"Since when?"

"Since my mother made it for you."

"She's very…efficient."

"She's very bossy."

"I heard that, Chance Richardson," Lila called out from the kitchen, and Chance grinned.

"She also has great hearing."

"You're right, I do. And what I hear is the two of you chattering like you have been all day. You don't have time. The receptionist squeezed Rayne in between patients. If you're not at the office on time, she can't guarantee the appointment." Lila walked into the room, Emma babbling happily in her arms.

Rayne took the baby, kissed her chubby cheek. "You look like you feel better, Little Miss."

"She ate rice cereal and banana and drank her bottle. Now we're ready to play. Right, darling?" Lila tickled the baby's belly, and Rayne smiled as her daughter's giggles filled the room.

She'd be in good hands.

Of course she would.

But the thought of leaving her made Rayne feel physically ill.

Or maybe the head injury was doing that.

"Here. Let me hold her while you go freshen up, okay? You need to walk out the door in ten minutes if you're going to be there on time."

Lila scooped Emma from Rayne's arms and set her on a blanket in the middle of the floor.

It looked like Lila had done the same thing many times. Looked like Emma was used to the books and toys and baby dolls scattered around on the blanket.

Looked like the two had a great routine going.

And why wouldn't they?

When Lila had explained how the house worked, she'd also told Rayne that she'd been Emma's babysitter for seven weeks.

Seven weeks Rayne couldn't remember.

She wiped damp palms on her jeans.

Standing around wasn't bringing the memories back.

It certainly wasn't helping her "freshen up."

"Need help up the stairs?" Chance asked, his low baritone shivering through her, his gaze drifting from the top of her head to her bare feet.

No.

Definitely not.

She did *not* need his help.

No men. Ever.

Rule two.

She wasn't going to break that one.

"I'll be fine." She walked past him, told herself that the man didn't smell as good as he looked. Spicy aftershave and outdoors and some indefinable thing that smelled like…

Chance.

Though how she'd know that when she couldn't remember where she'd been or what she'd done twenty-four hours ago, Rayne couldn't fathom.

Or didn't want to admit.

If she could have hurried, she would have, but going up the stairs with a throbbing head and an aching body wasn't easy. A door separated the apartment from the landing and she opened it, stepping into the cozy room Lila had showed her earlier. Familiar furniture. Familiar throw rug. A fireplace on one wall, her laptop sitting on a desk against another, toys strewn across the floor—the place had a lived-in feel that fit the life of a busy mother.

But aside from the furniture and throw that she'd brought with her from Arizona, it could have belonged to any busy mother. Nothing about it seemed familiar. Not the kitchen. Not the nursery. Not the charming master bedroom with its view of snow-covered mountains and fields.

Nothing.

No spark of memory.

She walked into the bathroom, ran a comb through wild curls, dabbed makeup over the dark bruise on her cheek. The other one was past hope. Green, blue and red with tinges of black, it rose off her forehead like a hump on the back of a camel.

Huge.

No camouflage in the world could hide it so she didn't bother trying, just swept gloss over her lips, mascara on her lashes.

Mascara?

Lip gloss?

To go the doctor?

What would be next?

Blush and perfume?

"Don't you dare, Rayne," she muttered at her reflection.

No blush. No perfume. No cute outfit to try to distract from the bruise on her head.

She was going to the doctor just the way she was, because she had no one to impress but herself.

No Michael to tell her that she looked a little pale, that her hair needed to be tamed, that she could stand to lose a few pounds.

No man.

Period.

"Rayne?" Chance called out, and she absolutely refused to admit that she glanced in the mirror one last time before she walked out of the bathroom to greet him.

He stood in the threshold of the open door, his dress shirt open at the collar, a tie hanging loose around his neck, and her heart did the unthinkable.

It jumped.

Stupid heart. Don't you know the rules?

"I'm ready."

"I think your feet are going to get a little cold if you go the way you are."

She glanced down.

Bare toes.

Great.

Glanced up.

Chance and his silver-blue eyes sparking with amusement.

Even better.

"I'll get socks." She ran as fast as her aching

body could carry her. Down the hall. Into her room. Fumbled through drawers until she found socks.

"Get yourself together, Rayne. He's a guy. You have plenty of guy friends. Just pretend he's one of them," she mumbled as she pulled socks on.

"Did you say something?" Chance called out from the living room.

"No." Not to him, anyway.

She did *not* look in the mirror over the dresser before she walked out of the room, didn't glance Chance's way as she grabbed boots from a shoe rack near the door and shoved her feet into them, did not allow her silly heart to jump and cheer when he put a hand on her shoulder to steady her.

"There. Now I'm really ready."

"Coat?" he asked, and she pulled one from the closet, tried to get her arms into the sleeves, but her body felt stiff and ill-used, as if she'd run a marathon, biked through the desert and swum the Atlantic Ocean all in the same day.

"Let me help." He took the coat from her hands, held it while she maneuvered her arms through the sleeves, his fingers sliding along her neck as he adjusted the collar, heat sparking everywhere he touched.

"Thanks. I guess the accident gave me more than a concussion. There isn't a muscle in my body that doesn't ache." She stepped back and took a deep steadying breath. Inhaled…

Him.

"I'll grab some pain relievers for you before we leave. Hopefully, they'll take the edge off." He seemed completely unaware of the heat that had passed between them.

Good.

She had way too much to worry about without *that* added to it. The both of them feeling things they shouldn't.

Or, at least, things *she* shouldn't.

"I have ibuprofen in my purse. I'll take it on the way to the doctor." She grabbed her purse, walked out onto the landing, ready to put distance between them.

She'd have to keep her guard up to protect herself and her daughter.

"Were you able to contact the Arizona police?" she asked as she made her way down the stairs.

"Yes."

"What did they say about Leon?"

"How about we talk about it in the car?"

She turned at the bottom of the stairs, tried to read his expression. "How about we talk about it now?"

"And miss your appointment? You're already running late." Lila carried Emma into the foyer. "Give your mommy a kiss. She has to go."

Emma reached for Rayne, her lip quivering.

"Don't cry, sweetie. I'll be back soon." Rayne took the baby from Lila's arms, the sick feeling she'd had earlier back.

She couldn't put her finger on what caused it, didn't know why she felt anxious. Obviously, Lila cared about the baby and would care *for* her, but Rayne couldn't shake the feeling of dread that filled her every time she thought about leaving.

The dream.

It had to be that.

And the man standing in the doorway of her hospital room.

Those things had her on edge, made her imagine danger where there wasn't any.

Emma cried in earnest as Rayne kissed her cheek, smoothed her red hair, tried to convince herself to hand the baby back to Lila.

"Maybe this isn't a good idea."

"Going to the doctor?" Chance asked, and Rayne shook her head.

"Leaving Emma. She isn't herself."

"You're not yourself, either, dear. Staying here with Emma isn't going to make you any better, and taking her with you is no solution, either. Can you imagine all the germs in the doctor's office this time of year? Just think of what Emma would be exposed to. I promise you, I'll care for her the same way I have for the past weeks—like she's my own child. Or grandchild." She smiled and Rayne knew she'd do exactly what she'd said.

"I know you will, Lila."

She did.

But she still didn't want to leave Emma.

She kissed the baby's cheek and handed her back to Lila, anyway. It was the best decision—she knew it—but that didn't make it easy.

"She'll be fine, Rayne. Come on. The sooner

we go, the sooner you can get back to her. Make sure you lock the door, okay, Mom?" Chance said, tugging Rayne into the frigid afternoon.

White snow. Gold sun. Deep green pine trees. Blue sky.

Beautiful.

On any other day, Rayne would have enjoyed the breathtaking landscape.

Today she just wanted to get to the doctor's office and get back to Emma.

Chance started the engine, but instead of driving away from the two-story farmhouse, he turned to face her. "She really will be okay. You know that, right?"

"Yes." Otherwise she'd never have left Emma.

"Then what are you so worried about?"

What *was* she worried about?

She couldn't put her finger on it, couldn't quite put a name to what she was feeling. Anxious, worried, scared.

"I just…"

"What?"

"Feel like there's something I should know. Something important."

"Something about Emma?"

"Yes. Maybe. I don't know." She sighed, frustrated with the void the car accident had left.

"So how about we work together and see what we can find out?"

Say no.

Tell him you can handle things yourself.

No men. Period. Remember?

"How do you suggest we do that?"

Say no.

"We'll start with your computer. One of the guys from Information Unlimited specializes in computer forensics. I'll take yours to him, and we'll see what he comes up with."

No.

No, no, no.

She knew exactly what she needed to say to avoid breaking rule number two.

Knew it.

"All right. Thanks."

And didn't say it.

Obviously, the accident had created more than a void in her memories—it had scrambled her brains.

SIX

Since when had avoiding someone included driving her to the doctor's office?

Since never. That's when.

But that's exactly what Chance was about to do.

Drive Rayne to the doctor. And more.

Talk to the police about a man who might be after her. Keep an eye out for dark, foreign-made trucks.

Help her access deleted computer files.

Get more involved in her life than he should.

He wasn't sure how he felt about that, but he knew he didn't have a choice. The police in Phoenix had confirmed what Chance had feared. Darren Leon hadn't reported to his probation officer the previous week and wasn't at his apartment. They were sending patrol officers to look for him, but he could be anywhere.

Including Spokane.

Rayne was injured and alone, with a baby dependent on her. She needed his help, and she'd get it, whether she tested his self-control or not.

"You're frowning," Rayne said as he pulled onto the highway.

"The police in Phoenix weren't helpful when it came to locating Leon. He didn't check in with his probation officer last week. They're not sure where he is."

"I was afraid of that."

"I've already contacted the Spokane County Sheriff's Department. They're getting Leon's rap sheet and mug shot. Hopefully, if he's in town, they'll spot him."

"That's like hoping for rain in the desert."

"Even in the desert it rains sometimes, so don't discount what can happen with a lot of work and prayer."

"I'm not discounting anything, but I'd feel a lot more comfortable if Leon was where I wanted him to be."

"The police in Phoenix said they didn't think he was a threat to anyone. No record up until the day he accosted you."

"That's what the defense attorney said. All I know is that Leon blamed me for the wreck he'd made of his life. I'd helped his wife find a new job and move to another state. A little too much alcohol and he snapped."

"Do you think he meant to harm you?"

"Then? Yes. Now that I know the gun wasn't loaded, I'm not sure. I didn't stick around to find out, though. As soon as Kane offered me the job here, I packed my bags and left town. I guess running from my trouble didn't keep it from finding me."

"We don't know for sure that the man in your hospital room was Leon."

"Trouble is trouble, Chance. No matter what name it wears, and all I've had for the past eight months is a boatload of it."

"What kind of trouble are we talking about?"

"Eight months ago, my best friend—Emma's mother—died. I took custody of Emma and cleaned out the apartment where she and Chandra lived. About a week later, the storage unit I put Chandra's stuff in was broken into. A month after that, I broke up with Michael and canceled our wedding. Then Leon threatened to kill me for convincing his wife to leave him."

"So all the trouble began after Chandra died?

"It seems that way. Up until then, my life was predictable. Dinner out on Friday. Lunch out on Tuesday. Church on Sunday and Wednesday."

"Nothing wrong with that." Though he didn't see Rayne as a regimented type. Couldn't really imagine her carrying a daily planner and ticking off her to-do list.

"Nothing right about it, either."

"So you moved here to shake things up?"

"I shook things up by getting rid of Michael and his daily planner and minute-by-minute schedule. No more sitting for two hours after church on Sunday going over our week. It was really quite freeing." The lightness in her voice couldn't hide the edge in her tone.

"You sound angry."

"Only with myself. I still don't know how I let myself fall in…" She stopped, and he knew he should let it go, let their conversation move on to other things.

Knew it, but didn't.

"Love?"

"Is that what it was? If so, love isn't all it's cracked up to be."

"Love is what we make it. It's the effort we put into the relationships we're building."

"Have you ever been in love, Chance? Heart-pounding, soul-searing love, I mean. Not high-school-crush love."

"I thought I was. Thought it enough to plan a future and get married."

"You're married?"

"*Was* married. Jessica died three years ago. We were separated for nearly a year before that. As I said, love is the effort you put into the relationships you're building. I guess neither of us put enough into what we had."

"I'm sorry."

"Me, too. Jessica had a drug problem. I was away a lot working as an army chaplain. Those two things didn't go well together." If he could go back, he'd do things differently, spend more time with his wife, listen more carefully. All the things he'd done as a chaplain, he'd have used to make his marriage work.

It wouldn't have been enough. He knew that. Jessica had been steeped in addiction when they met. He'd just been too blinded by her beauty and sophistication, her brittle charm to see it. All his efforts couldn't have changed her, but they would have changed his feelings about himself, would have prevented the guilt that never seemed far away when he thought about Jessica.

He pulled into a space in front of the doctor's office, his failure as real and ugly and hard as it had been the day he'd learned that Jessica had died of a drug overdose.

"We can't change the people we love. We want to, we think we can, we try so hard to make them into who we think they can be, but only God can change a heart. Unless your wife wanted things to be different, there was nothing you could do." Rayne touched his hand, her fingers skimming over his knuckles before she pulled back.

A simple touch, but it hit him hard, stole his breath, made him forget all the reasons why relationships weren't for him.

"I could have been there for her. I could have found a way to make her a priority over my job." He could have done the same with his father and brother, but he hadn't been there for them, either. Missed birthdays. Missed holidays. Missed moments that he couldn't get back.

As he looked into Rayne's eyes, he couldn't help wondering if this was his chance at redemption. His chance to prove that he could be there for someone.

His chance to give the dream a second shot. Family and laughter and love.

"Come on. We'd better get inside. If you miss your appointment, my mother will have my hide." He got out of the car, took a deep breath of cold, crisp air, desperate to clear his head. Maybe he could help Rayne. Maybe he could even find the redemption he was so desperate for.

What he wouldn't find, what he refused to even look for, was love.

He'd tried for the dream. Failed. He didn't plan to try again. All his mother's hints about marriage and kids had fallen on deaf ears. No wife. No kids. Those things simply weren't for him.

At least that's what he'd been telling himself for three years. Sometimes, though, he wanted more than his empty cottage. Sometimes he wanted someone to come home to.

He frowned, taking Rayne's arm as they crossed the icy pavement. He'd help her because it was the right thing to do, but he wouldn't fall for her.

She moved past him as he held the door, glanced his way, her misty eyes filled with a hundred things he couldn't read. Shouldn't want to read, but did.

There was something about her.

Something he couldn't ignore, no matter how hard he tried. Something he couldn't deny, no matter how much he wanted to.

"I'll check in." She moved across the small lobby, her gait stiff, her muscles tight, pain etched in the hollows of her cheeks and in the deep circles beneath her eyes. Tough. Strong. A fighter. She was all those things, but there was a gentleness to her, too. A softness that put everyone she met at ease.

He turned away, uncomfortable with his thoughts. He'd dated a few women since Jessica's death, but none had compelled him the way Rayne did. None had made him want more than he should.

Outside, the nearly empty parking lot gleamed in the sunlight. The few vehicles in it parked close to the building. All except for one. A dark truck. Foreign. No license plate. Not one on its front end, anyway.

Had it been there when they'd pulled in?

Chance didn't remember seeing it.

He stepped outside, adrenaline shooting through him as the truck sped to the edge of the parking lot and out onto the main road. No plate on the back, either.

A coincidence that it looked like the truck Fred had described?

Probably.

But Chance didn't like loose ends. He wanted everything tied up nice and neat.

"Is every okay?" Rayne stepped outside, her gaze following the truck as it disappeared.

"Fine."

"Then, why are you standing out here watching a truck drive away?"

"Just wondering who was in it."

"Because?"

"My neighbor saw a similar truck on our road last night."

"You think it's the same truck?"

"I don't know, but I'd like to find out."

"I suppose you have an idea about how to do that?"

"No, but now that I've seen the truck, I'll know if I see it again." He led her back into the office, wishing he had a license plate to go on.

Her cell phone rang as they walked back into the office, and she glanced at the number, frowned, shoved the phone back into her purse.

"Not someone you want to talk to?" he asked.

"It was Michael, and I really don't have the time or patience to deal with him right now."

"Give me the phone. I'll take care of it for you." Happily. Chance might not be planning to fall for Rayne, but that didn't mean he was going to let her ex harass her.

"I'm a grown woman with a child and a job and a life. I'm perfectly capable of handling things myself."

"But you didn't." He pointed out the obvious and she scowled.

"Just because I didn't handle it your way doesn't mean I didn't take care of the problem."

"Ignoring a problem never makes it go away."

"I don't plan to ignore it forever. Just…for now."

"Rayne—"

"Chance, I appreciate the help you've been giving me. I really do, but—"

"Is this one of those verbal Dear John letters? *'I like you, but things just aren't working out'?*" he cut in, surprising a chuckle out of her.

"Now it's not. You've ruined the moment."

"Sorry about that, but we don't have to take things so seriously. I'm helping you until you're well. That's all. Neither of us is looking for anything more. Just two people giving each other a hand. There's nothing wrong with that."

"There is when one person is doing all the helping and the other person is doing all the being helped."

"Is that what this is about? Me helping you too much?"

"Not your helping. My needing help. I don't want to rely on you or anyone else. Not the way I did when I was dating Michael, letting him make all the decisions about where we were going, when and what we'd wear. I just want to live my life as me. Decide for myself what's best—and whether I want to accept someone's help or not."

"I don't see how my helping you can keep you from making your own decisions." He studied her face, looked for the truth in her eyes, but all he saw was fatigue, fear and the same confusion he felt every time their gazes met.

All his plans, all his dreams out the window with one look into her misty eyes. Yeah. He understood all about confusion.

"It's not your helping that I'm worried about. It's what could come of all the help, all the time spent together, that's worrying me." She looked away, breaking the connection, clearing the air of whatever was between them.

"You've got nothing to worry about then. Neither of us wants another relationship, right?"

"Right."

"For now, you need my help. In a couple of days, maybe a week, you won't. When that happens, I'll back out of your life as easily as I entered it."

"But—"

"What?" he asked, but he knew. She felt what he did, the energy and connection that had been there from the moment she'd walked into Kane Dougherty's boardroom to meet the Information Unlimited staff and they'd looked into each other's eyes.

"I just don't want to make another mistake."

"Letting me help you isn't a mistake, Rayne. It isn't going to change you any more than you want to be changed by it."

"That's the problem, Chance. What I want. Which is a whole lot more than what I should."

"Rayne Sampson?" A nurse stepped into the waiting area, and Rayne hurried away.

Not a backward glance.

Not a quick goodbye.

Nothing but her words hanging in the air.

What I want. Which is a whole lot more than what I should.

Yeah. He understood that, too.

Hopefully, wanting more wouldn't make a liar out of him, saying he could walk away when this was over.

He pulled out his cell phone, dialed the sheriff and left a message. Then dialed Kai Parker's number. A deputy with the Spokane County

Sheriff's Department, he'd helped out with a few of Kane's investigations. Hopefully, he'd be willing to help again.

"Deputy Parker. What can I do for you?"

"No need to sound so formal, Kai."

"I was wondering when you'd call. Heard there was some action going on in your life."

"Not mine. Rayne Sampson's. She—"

"Lives in your mom's attic apartment, has partial amnesia and might have a killer after her. Heard the story from the sheriff. Want to tell me something new?"

"My neighbor saw a truck drive down our road last night. He said it took half an hour for the driver to realize he'd hit a dead end and turn around."

"Someone visiting your mom?"

"That's what he thought, but she was at the hospital."

"What kind of truck?"

"Dark. Foreign."

"Only a few thousand of those in the county."

"A few thousand plus the one I saw in front of the doctor's office a few minutes ago."

"You get a plate number?"

"No plates."

"Guy might get pulled over for that."

"If he does, I'd like to know who he is."

"I'll let you know if it happens. Anything else?"

"The sheriff was running a phone number for me. I tried to call, but he wasn't in."

"I heard about that, too, and I have an answer for you. Probably not one you're going to like. The number belongs to a prepaid cell phone. No way to trace it, but the sheriff did find out where it was sold."

"Arizona?"

"Bingo. Buyer paid for it with cash. Phoenix P.D. is checking to see if the person who bought it matches a description of Darren Leon. I'll give you a call as soon as we know something new."

"I appreciate it, Kai."

"No problem. I'll keep in touch." Kai hung up and Chance paced across the small room, stared out into the parking lot again. The likelihood the truck would be spotted and pulled over was slim. The likelihood that it was the same truck that Fred had seen was even slimmer. But he had to try.

Never there.

Too busy for anything but work.

Good at your job but not good with people.

Old words thrown at him by Jessica the day she'd walked out. Underlying them was just enough truth to make them cling long after she'd gone.

Not there for Jessica.

Not there the night his brother and father died.

Not there nearly enough.

He couldn't change that, but he wouldn't make the same mistake again.

As long as Rayne needed his help, he'd spend the time and energy it took to give it.

And then, when it was over, he'd do exactly what he'd said. He'd walk out of her life.

He just wasn't sure how easy the walking would be.

SEVEN

Remember rule number two?

No men. Ever.

Well, you're about to break it, Rayne Sampson. One more look in those blue-gray eyes and it'll all be over. Rule number two broken.

"I am not going to break rule number two," Rayne muttered, and the nurse looked up from the chart she was writing on.

"Pardon me?"

"Nothing. Just talking to myself."

"Do you do that often or is this something new?" The nurse looked to be about twelve years old, black hair pulled into a silky ponytail, her green eyes wide with concern.

"I've been doing it most of my life."

"Oh. Okay. That's fine then. The doctor will be with you in just a moment."

"Thanks." She waited until the nurse walked out the door and eased off the gurney, her head throbbing in time with her heart. She wanted to be anywhere but where she was, but mostly, she wanted to be home.

Not home in her new apartment.

Home in Arizona, her parents close by. Her friends. All the things she'd left behind. Community and connections. All the stuff that made a place home.

Now she was drifting. No memories to anchor her in Spokane. Nothing solid to hold on to.

Just Emma, Lila, Chance.

Chance.

He was a problem. No doubt about it.

She'd already broken one rule because of him, and she was sliding straight into breaking rule number two.

Stupid rules.

Stupid heart.

I'll back out of your life as easily as I entered it.

That's what he'd said, and her foolish, fickle heart hadn't been happy about how blithely those words had come, how sincere he'd looked when he'd said them.

He'd back out of *her* life easily, but would *she* be able to back away from *him?*

Yes. She would. She could.

Couldn't she?

Something about Chance grabbed her attention and held it. Made her want to forget her three cardinal rules for heart-healthy living.

Someone knocked on the door, and it swung open, a tall, bearded man walking in. "Ms. Sampson? I'm Dr. Jeffries. I hear you've been in an accident."

"Yes." Rayne explained quickly, wishing she'd gone with her gut and stayed with Emma. No intrusive questions from a doctor she didn't know and who didn't know her, no waiting for a diagnosis she'd already received at the hospital, no ride back to the house with Chance.

There he was again.

Right where he shouldn't be.

At the forefront of her mind.

Pitiful, considering all the other things she had to worry about.

The doctor flashed a light in her eyes, asked questions she couldn't answer, checked her reflexes and her heart.

"Well, Ms. Sampson, aside from the bruising and soreness, you seem to be healthy."

"And the amnesia?"

"Could be permanent, but most people regain at least some of their memories over time."

"How *much* time?"

"Some people regain their memories in a few hours. For others, it takes weeks. Even months. The good news is that you're alive. You can go on to build plenty of new memories. That's not an opportunity everyone has." His reminder hit home, the truth of how close she'd come to dying setting in as he said goodbye.

If Chance hadn't been out looking for her, how long would it have been before she was found?

Too long.

As much as she didn't want to have him in her life, she couldn't deny what he'd done for her. What he continued to do for her.

"Knock, knock." Chance stepped into the room, his dark hair falling over his forehead, his eyes seeming to glow in his deeply tanned face. He looked like a man who spent more time outdoors than indoors, his broad hands nicked and scarred, his muscles formed by manual labor rather than time in the gym.

Handsome.

Caring.

Easy to talk to.

All the things any woman would be happy to have in a partner.

A woman who wasn't her, she reminded herself firmly.

"What are you doing in here?"

"The nurse told me you were done. I figured I'd escort you out."

"I've been escorting myself for a long time, Chance. I'm sure I can find my own way out."

"Probably, but I had some news to share." He helped her into her coat, his knuckles scraping along her jaw as he pulled her collar up around her neck.

"I'm not two years old, Chance. I can handle this." She stepped back, her skin hot from his touch.

"I figured you could."

"So what's the news?" *Keep talking, keep walking, keep acting like his touch had no effect on you.*

"Remember the phone number you found on your cell phone? The police were able to trace the number to a prepaid phone."

"Do they know who it belonged to?"

"Unfortunately, no. But they do know where it was purchased. Want to take a wild guess?"

"Arizona?"

"Exactly."

"Great. Except knowing where it was purchased doesn't tell us who made the call."

"We'll figure it out."

"You have a lot more confidence than I do."

"It's not confidence. It's faith."

Faith?

She'd always thought she had plenty of faith, but over the years her passion for the things of God had faded. School, job, life, relationships—they'd all vied for her attention. Church had become one more thing to do. Prayer something she did quickly and in passing. God was there. She knew it. That had become enough.

It shouldn't have.

She'd realized it after she'd broken up with Michael, but hadn't quite known how to grasp what she'd lost.

"You're quiet." Chance pressed a hand to her back, urging her out into the biting cold. Clouds blanketed the sky, painting everything in grayish light.

"Just thinking about how easy it is for faith to get lost in the busyness of life."

"Not lost, Rayne. Just hidden for a while."

"It's the same thing, isn't it?"

"The way I see it, if something is lost it's past hope. Something that is hidden simply needs to be uncovered." He helped her into the SUV, his hand on her waist, warm and strong and comforting.

Just like his words.

She felt filled up with him, with the words, with everything she shouldn't want.

Faith. Love. Home. Family. She'd thought she could have that all with Michael, but she'd been so wrong. How could she trust herself to make the right call now?

That was easy enough to answer—she couldn't.

"You're a dangerous man, Chance Richardson," she said without meaning to, and he looked into her eyes, looked so long and so deep that she wondered if either of them would ever look away.

"I was thinking the same about you, Goldilocks." He stepped back, closed the door, locking her into the SUV, her heart thudding with all the things she shouldn't feel.

Rule number two breaking into a million pieces.

Her cell phone rang, and she grabbed it, desperate for a distraction. "Hello?"

"Finally. I've been trying to call you all day." Michael's voice filled her ear, carrying the weight of his disapproval.

"Why?"

"To see how you're feeling. Despite what you might think, Rayne, I do still care."

"I wish you wouldn't."

"Sarcasm doesn't suit you."

"I wasn't being sarcastic." Cold air whipped into the SUV as Chance climbed in.

"Then you were being rude."

"I'm sorry you feel that way. I wasn't trying to be rude. I was just stating the facts."

"The facts are, you were injured in a car accident and you're out in the middle of nowhere. No family to help. No friends."

"No you?" She was sure that was what he was thinking. Michael had always had an overblown sense of his importance in their relationship. It had only taken her three years to realize it.

"Look, I didn't call to argue. I called because

your parents said you asked them not to fly out and—"

"You spoke with my parents."

"Yes. Does that bother you?"

"Michael—"

"Tell him you're not in the mood to listen to him whine." Chance said.

"Shhhhh."

"Rayne, if you're not going to give your full attention to our conversation, I may as well end it. As you know, I have a busy schedule."

"Of course I know about your busy schedule. Our entire dating relationship had to be worked around it."

"That's not fair."

"Look, I've got a splitting headache. I'm exhausted. I don't want to argue with you. I'm fine. I'll continue to be fine. You don't need to call me again to check on me."

"You've changed, Rayne."

"Only back into the person I was before I met you. Goodbye, Michael." She hung up, pressed a hand to her throbbing head.

What was the man thinking, calling her over and over again?

"He's trying to win you back." Chance's remark wasn't a question, but Rayne answered anyway.

"No. He just wants to make sure I'm okay."

"How many of your friends have called today?"

"A few. They left messages, but I haven't had a chance to call them back."

"And how many times have each of them called?

"Once."

"Exactly. He's trying to win you back."

She laughed. No way would Michael try to get her back.

She came with Emma, and Emma was not in his plans.

"What's so funny?"

"The idea that he'd want to get back together with me. We broke up because of him. He didn't want to take responsibility for Emma. He thought I should find her a good home with a family better suited to her than we were."

"Sounds…cold."

"I thought so. He told me to make a choice. Emma or him. I chose Emma."

"Good. The guy didn't deserve either of you."

"That's what my folks said. It's what my brother and sister-in-law said. It's what everyone said."

"But?"

"I kept wondering why no one had told me that before. All those years wasted on a guy who wasn't worth it, and not one person bothered to tell me I was making a mistake."

"They wanted you to be happy. He seemed to make you happy. That's all that mattered to them."

He was right. Of course he was.

Her family and friends had accepted Michael because of her. They'd put up with his arrogance and his busy schedule because she'd said she was happy with him.

"You're really good at this, Chance."

"What?"

"Listening. Talking. Saying the right thing."

"I've had a lot of practice. I worked as an army chaplain."

"What brought you back here?"

"My brother and father were killed in a car accident. When they died, I came home to help my mother with the farm and the orchards. Of course, she didn't need it nearly as much as I'd been imagining."

"How long ago was that?"

"Two years."

"It must have been hard."

"Very. I had a lot of regrets. I still do, but you can't go back, can you?" He offered a quick smile, the pain in his voice palpable.

"I know about regret, Chance. And I know that living in it doesn't do any good." She touched his arm, his muscles tense beneath her palm.

"I'm not living in it. Most days." He covered her hand, the gesture becoming something more, seconds ticking by, breath held, waiting for one or the other to pull away.

Pull away!

Now!

She slid her hand from beneath his, warmth lingering as silence filled the SUV, the weight of that one touch heavy on her heart.

She couldn't break rule two.

Couldn't.

So why did she want to so badly?

She scowled, frustrated with herself, with Chance, with Michael. With her whole messed-up life.

"Need a punching bag?" Chance broke the silence, his words clearing the air, chasing away the warmth of his touch, the heavy weight of broken dreams and secret yearnings.

"I'm fine."

"Then why do you look like you want to take someone's head off?"

Good question.

How should she answer?

Because my life is chaos and I don't know why?

Because my ex keeps calling, and it reminds me of all the foolish dreams I'd invested in him?

Because I don't want to fall for you, but I am?

"Rayne?" Chance pulled up in front of his mother's farmhouse, parked the car.

"As I said, I'm fine."

"Is that what you always do?" he asked, shifting so they were face-to-face.

"What?"

"Pretend that everything is fine even when it isn't? You've had a rough twenty-four hours. You're exhausted. Your ex is driving you nuts. It's not a crime to be annoyed."

"Good, because you're really annoying me, too." She opened the door, shivering as cold air whipped her hair and slapped her bruised cheek.

"I guess you're going to tell me why?" Chance asked, the amusement in his voice unmistakable.

And irresistible.

But she would *not* smile, wouldn't even crack a grin, because that would mean giving in to more of what she felt for him, and she'd already done enough of that.

"Actually, I'm not."

"Then how about I guess?"

"I'd rather you wouldn't."

"Chicken."

"Look, you want the truth? I'll give it to you." She swung around to face him, the wind whipping hair into her eyes. "I just dumped my fiancé, and I don't want another relationship. I don't even want to tiptoe on the edge of another relationship. When I'm with you, I seem to forget that."

There. She'd said it.

She turned, ready to go into the house, get Emma, bring her up to the apartment. Just the two of them. The way she'd planned it when she'd left Phoenix.

"Rayne." He didn't touch her, didn't do anything but say her name, but she felt helpless to move away.

"I have to go in. Emma needs me."

"I know, but there's something I want to say first." His hands slid up her arms, cupped her shoulders, and everything in her stilled as she looked into his face, saw all that she felt reflected there.

"Don't."

"Tiptoeing or not, we're going somewhere together. Wherever we end up, who you are is exactly who I want you to be. No changing. No hiding. No doing anything differently. You being you is plenty." He skimmed her cheek with his knuckles, and she shivered, turning away, half running, half limping up the porch stairs and into the house.

Rule number two.

Broken.

Only rule number three stood between her and disaster, and there was absolutely no way she was going to break that one.

She hoped.

EIGHT

He'd crossed the line, and he knew it.

What Chance didn't know was whether or not he regretted it.

She'd looked so frustrated and upset that the words had just spilled out. The *truth* had spilled out, since he'd meant every word. He just wasn't sure he was ready to handle what might come of it.

He followed Rayne into the house, let the warmth of home wash over him.

"You're back! And none too soon. We're in for another winter storm tonight. Come sit down and get warm. There's a fire going in the living room. Chance, maybe you can get one started in Rayne's apartment before you leave."

His mother walked out of the kitchen, Emma in her arms.

"It's okay. I used to camp with my brother when I was little. He taught me how to start a fire." Rayne responded, her voice tight, and Chance knew Lila noticed.

Her gaze jumped from Rayne to him and back again. Then she shot him a look he hadn't seen since he'd broken her favorite vase the summer he turned twelve.

"I'm innocent, Mom."

"I didn't say anything."

"You didn't have to. You've perfected *the look*."

"It's a gift." She turned her attention to Rayne. "How did the appointment go?"

"Fine. Aside from bumps and bruises, I'm healthy. My memory should return at some point, but the doctor doesn't know when." Rayne took Emma, nuzzling the baby's red curls. "How was she while I was gone?"

"A little fussy, but mostly good as gold."

"Still fussy? Maybe she's teething." Rayne frowned, pressed her lips to Emma's forehead.

"It's possible. Both my boys fussed nonstop when they were teething. Especially Chance. Of course, he was just fussy period."

"Not true. I was the most pleasant baby in the world. You've told me that a dozen times."

"Only because I didn't want to crush your delicate feelings." Lila smiled, and Rayne laughed, the tension easing from her face.

"I'm not sure I think it's funny." But he did enjoy hearing Rayne laugh.

Which was only a small part of the problem he seemed to be having with her.

"*I* do," Rayne responded, carrying Emma into the living room and dropping down into the rocking chair. Despite her laughter, she looked tired, her skin pale beneath the bruises.

"You're exhausted, dear. I'll make you a nice cup of chamomile tea. Dinner will be ready in fifteen minutes. We'll eat in here. That way, you and Miss Emma don't have to move." Lila hurried from the room, and Chance did what he needed to. Not apologize. He wouldn't apologize for telling the truth. He had to clear the air. Get the conversation moving between them again. There was too much at stake for anything else.

"I didn't mean to make you uncomfortable, Rayne."

"I'm too tired to discuss it, so let's just pretend neither of us said anything and move on, okay?" She rocked Emma, patting her back rhythmically, her gaze on the window and the gray afternoon beyond it.

"That's not the way I work."

"It's going to have to be, because I can't do anything else right now." She met his eyes, forced a smile.

"Okay."

"Just like that?"

"Just like that. For now."

"You make it really difficult, Chance." Rayne stood, walked to the window, Emma lying against her shoulder.

"I make what really difficult?"

"To not break rule number three."

"Rule number three?" He joined her at the window.

"I made three rules after I broke up with Michael. Don't rely on anyone. No men. Ever. And…" Her voice trailed off, and she shrugged. "Well, let's just say I've broken the first two rules already. Now I'm nose-diving toward rule three, and I don't know how to stop myself."

"Then maybe you don't really want to."

"Maybe not, but for Emma's sake I need to. She's my first priority."

"That's the way it should be."

"See? There you go again. Making it difficult. And here I go, talking about this...*stuff* when I said I didn't want to. There are so many more important things I need to worry about. Like, who made that phone call last night? Who was in the hospital room with me? Where is Leon?"

"We'll figure it all out eventually. How about, for tonight, you let that be enough?"

"I—" Headlights flashed on the pavement, shimmering in ice and snow, cutting off Rayne's words before she could finish.

Chance tensed, watching as the vehicle drove into view. A small pickup. Dark. No license plates.

"Get down!" he shouted as the driver's window opened. The driver was briefly visible. Dark hair. No. Not hair. A hood. Eyes.

Rayne dropped to the floor, shielding Emma's body, and he tried to shield them both, his body covering theirs as something exploded. Glass shattered and fell like rain, flames shooting up the wall near his head.

Emma screaming.

Rayne coughing.

Frigid wind and brutal heat. Snow and fire.

"Move!" Chance grabbed Rayne's arm, hauled her to her feet, fire climbing up the curtains, eating the wall, smoke filling the room. Emma coughing, gagging, screaming.

He had to get them out. Get his mother out.

Then he had to see if the truck driver was still around.

"Dear God! What happened?" Lila ran into the room, her eyes wide with fear.

"Into the mudroom. Let's move!" Chance shouted. No time for explanations. No time for anything but escape.

He held Rayne's arm, took his mother's hand, pulled them through the kitchen and into the mudroom. No smoke there. Yet.

"Wait here. Both of you. Don't come out until I give you the okay." He opened the door, paused when Rayne grabbed his arm.

"Where are you going?"

"I need to make sure the truck driver is gone. If he's waiting—"

"You can't go out there. What if he *is* waiting?"

"What are you two talking about? The house is on fire. We can't stand around arguing!" Lila was as close to panic as Chance had ever seen her, and he squeezed her hand.

"I'll explain everything when I get back. Just stay here until I give you an all-clear." Chance threw the warning over his shoulder as he jogged down the deck steps and raced around the side of the house, the smoke alarm shrieking in his ears, echoing Emma's panicked screams. Everything faded as he ran into the front yard, saw the empty road.

No truck. No assailant. Nothing but flames shooting through the porch roof and lighting up the sky.

Chance dialed 9-1-1 and shouted his mother's address into his cell phone as he raced back around the house, up the stairs to the mudroom. His mother hovered in the doorway, Emma in her arms.

"Where's Rayne?" he shouted above the shrieking smoke alarm and the crying baby.

"She went back in to call for help. She hasn't come back out yet. I should have told her not to go. I should—"

"Take the baby outside. I'll find her." He darted past his mother, but she grabbed his arm, stopped him before he could run into the kitchen.

"Be careful. I can't lose someone else I love."

"I'll be out in a minute. Whatever you do, don't come after us. Okay?"

That was the rule, right?

Don't go back in.

Let the firefighters do the rescuing.

That was the rule, but he'd been a rule breaker for more years than he'd been a rule follower. Even if he hadn't been, he wouldn't have waited, wouldn't have risked Rayne's life to save his own. He plunged into the smoke-filled kitchen.

Five steps across the room.

Through the doorway and into the living room.

Fire still burning in the fireplace, black smoke pouring in through the broken window, flames crawling up the wall.

"Rayne!"

Where was she?

He coughed, choking on smoke and ash. Took another step, saw movement in the darkness.

A shadow emerged from the smoke. Someone grabbed his arm.

"You're supposed to be outside looking for

the bad guy." Rayne yelled, the words ending on a hacking cough.

"And you're supposed to be waiting in the mudroom. Come on." He dragged her back through the smoke.

"I had to call for help. The phone in the kitchen didn't work, so I had to get my cell phone."

"I have a phone, and I've already called for help." Cold air cooled his heated skin as he and Rayne stepped outside.

Fresh air tinged with smoke.

He inhaled, coughed up a lungful of soot.

"Thank goodness you're both okay." His mother hurried toward them, Emma in her arms, smoke and snow swirling around them.

"Here," Rayne said. "I grabbed the diaper bag while I was inside. Let's get her covered up." Rayne unzipped the bag, pulled out a blanket and wrapped it around her daughter. Apparently completely oblivious to the fact that she'd put herself in danger for a phone she didn't need and a diaper bag filled with replaceable things.

"We need to talk." He grabbed her hand,

tugged her a few feet away from his mother and Emma.

"You can forget the lecture. I know you think that what I did was stupid."

"That wasn't the word I planned to use."

"I guess you're going to tell me what word you *did* plan to use?" She stared him down, tendrils of blond hair falling around her pale face, her eyes hot and dark.

"Foolish. Foolhardy. Rash. Reckless. Take your pick."

"Right. Because when you run outside to face down the guy who bombed your mother's house, it's heroic. When I run to get a phone to call for help and potentially save your hide, it's foolish, foolhardy and reckless."

"You forgot rash."

"This isn't funny, Chance."

"You're right. It's not. But I went outside to make sure it was safe for you, Mom and Emma. I wasn't going after anyone. If you'd done what I asked and stayed inside, you wouldn't have put both our lives at risk."

"We're both fine. So how about we just agree we both did what we thought we had to and leave it at that." She stalked away, taking

Emma from his mother and hugging her close, blond hair falling over her face and spilling onto the blanket that covered the baby.

You make it difficult, she'd said.

She made it difficult, too.

To keep his distance.

To pretend he'd be able to turn his back and walk away.

To act as if he didn't care more than he should.

Sirens screamed, the sound mixing with the muted wail of the smoke alarm, the whipping wind and Emma's frantic cries. Poor kid. Scared, cold, tired.

He put his hand on her back, his fingers brushing Rayne's. "Is she okay?"

"I think so." Her voice shook and tears tracked through the soot that stained her face.

"You're crying."

"My eyes are watering."

"You're crying."

"Okay. I'm crying. Happy?" She wiped at the tears, smearing black across her cheeks.

"I'll never be happy when you're hurting." He knew he shouldn't. Knew it. But he pulled her into his arms anyway, Emma sandwiched between them.

"Are you both okay? I've never been so scared in my life as I was when you went back into the house." His mother hovered a few feet away, her gaze on the smoke billowing from the roof of the house.

"Emma and I are fine. How about you, Chance?" Rayne stepped back, not meeting his eyes as she asked the question.

Uncomfortable.

So was he, but he felt helpless to do anything but move in the direction they seemed to be going.

"I'm fine. Let's go around front. You guys can sit in my truck. It'll be warmer in there."

"Good idea." His mother offered a hollow smile, and Chance slid his arm around her waist.

"It'll be okay."

"I know. It's just…all my memories are in that house."

"All your memories are in your heart. Nothing can take them from you," Chance said quietly.

"I'm so sorry, Lila. This is all my fault. If

you lose everything, I'll never forgive myself." Rayne slid her arm around Lila's shoulders, and they walked, side by side by side into the front yard.

"How is this your fault, dear? Did you light a match and set my house on fire?"

"No, but—"

"Then I don't want to hear another word about it. Besides, it looks like the fire is dying. There will be smoke damage and water damage, but I think this old place will hold up." Lila stared at the facade of the house, and Chance had to agree. The fire seemed to be burning itself out, the accumulated snow from the previous day melting from the porch and roof and falling onto the flames.

"I think you're right, Mom. Come on. You three need to get into the truck."

A fire truck raced toward the house as Chance helped his mother into the front seat, handed her the keys. "Go ahead and turn it on. I'll take care of things out here."

He started to open the passenger door, but Rayne put a hand on his arm.

"Chance, no matter what your mother says,

we both know this is my fault. I should never have come here."

"The only person who is at fault is the person who tossed the bomb."

"Is that what it was?"

"I don't know, but I want to find out. Get in the truck before you and Emma freeze. I'll let you know what happened as soon as I know."

She looked like she wanted to argue, but Emma whimpered, and she nodded instead.

"Okay, but even if the house is habitable, I want to find another place to stay. I don't want to put your mother in any more danger than I already have."

"I'll find a place for you."

"Thanks." She climbed into the truck, and he closed the door, all three women safely tucked away.

Now he could concentrate on gathering the clues, piecing them together.

A marked police car sped up the drive and skidded to a halt a few yards away. An officer jumped out. Five-ten. Lean runner's build. Cropped dark hair. Kai Parker.

"Hey, man. Looks like you've got more trouble than you bargained for." He glanced at the smoldering front porch, met Chance's eyes.

"Looks like it."

"The way dispatch called it, someone threw an explosive at the house?"

"That's right."

"You tell the fire department?"

"When I called it in."

"Anyone hurt?"

"No. Thank God."

"Don't know how much I'd be thanking Him for this." Kai gestured at the house, the brigade of firefighters spraying it down, the snow pouring from the sky.

"Things could be a lot worse. I'm thanking Him for not letting them be."

"How about we just focus on figuring out what went down here. Can you tell me anything about the guy who tossed the explosive?"

"His truck had no license plates. Looked like the truck I saw earlier. I got a glimpse of the perp, but he had a hood hiding his face."

"I'll put an APB out on the truck. Did you get a look at the make?"

"Mitsubishi."

"That'll help. Any chance this isn't about Rayne and Darren Leon?"

"My mother doesn't have any enemies, so I doubt the perp was going after her."

"You're a private investigator. I'm sure you've made an enemy or two. And it's possible there are other abusive husbands out there with grudges against Rayne for helping their wives get away."

"Maybe, but let's not look for zebras when a horse is standing right in front of us."

"The horse being Leon?"

"Exactly."

"We're searching for him here. Phoenix P.D. is still searching for him there. I've got no doubt we're going to find him."

"But will you find him before he accomplishes his goal?" Chance asked, but there wasn't time for Kai to answer before Rayne stepped up beside him.

"How is everything going?" Her teeth chattered, and she rubbed her hands up and down her arms.

"I thought you were waiting in the truck."

"I wanted to see what was going on."

"You don't have a coat. You're going to freeze."

"You don't have a coat, either."

"She's got a point, Chance. Here. Throw these over your shoulders." Kai pulled blankets from the trunk of his car, handed one to each of them.

"Deputy Kai Parker, this is Rayne Sampson. Rayne, Kai is an old friend of mine. He's also an excellent police officer."

"It's nice to meet you, Deputy Parker." Rayne offered her hand, the subtle trembling of her arm nearly unnoticeable.

But Chance noticed.

Just as he noticed her pallid skin, her discomfort, the way she shifted from foot to foot. Impatient, anxious, scared.

"Nice to meet you, too. Though I could think of better circumstances to do it under. How about we have a seat in my cruiser while the fire crew finishes up? We can talk in there."

"That's fine," Rayne said, allowing herself to be led to the cruiser. Chance followed, waiting while Kai helped her into the passenger seat. Another police cruiser pulled up before he could shut the door.

"That's the sheriff," Kai said. "I'll check in with him and be right back. Just hold tight, okay?" He hurried across the space that separated the cars, and Chance leaned down, looked into Rayne's face.

"You doing okay?"

"Aside from the fact that I feel terrible about your mother's house? Yes."

"I told you that it's not your fault."

"It doesn't feel that way to me. If Leon followed me up here, if he's the reason for all this…" She shook her head, winced and rubbed her forehead.

"Headache?"

"Not any worse than it's been."

"Once Kai finishes interviewing you, I'll call Kane. Between the two of us, we should be able to find a safe place for you and Emma to stay for the night. You'll feel better once you get some sleep."

"So I'm running again, right? From Arizona to Spokane. From Spokane to wherever you and Kane think I should go. I wish I believed all the running would keep trouble from finding me, but I don't."

"All we need it to do is buy us some time."

"I'm not sure it's going to do that, either."

"Things will be okay."

"You can't know that."

"No, I guess I can't."

"At least you're honest about it. Deputy Parker is on his way back. I'll talk to him. Then, I'll see if the fire crew will let me in to get a few things. If Emma and I have to run again, it would be nice to bring some of her favorite things along." Chance knew there was nothing he could say that would make her feel better. Nothing he could say that would change the dejected slope of her shoulders, the drawn look on her face.

He wanted to change things for her, though.

Wanted to be able to offer her the happily-ever-after that he hadn't been able to give to Jessica. Wanted to succeed where he had failed before. Wanted more than anything to believe he could.

He watched as Rayne settled deeper into Kai's patrol car, then dialed Kane's number, praying desperately that God would help him save Rayne and Emma and help him find the redemption he so desperately sought.

NINE

Two hours, ten minutes, fifteen seconds.

That's how long it had been since Kane had driven Rayne away from Lila's house. From Lila. From Chance. From the fire fighters who had still been milling around the burnt porch.

Two hours, ten minutes and sixteen seconds. Seventeen.

Emma whimpered, drawing Rayne's attention away from her watch.

"Shh. Go back to sleep, sweetie." She smoothed Emma's hair, wishing she could cuddle her close.

"Is she okay?" Kane asked, his deep voice more familiar than his face had been when he'd shown up at the farmhouse. She'd spoken to him several times before she'd moved to Spokane, interviewing over the phone for the job as family advocate for his private investigation service. Her sister-in-law, Skylar, a private detective with the firm, had recommended her for the job, and Rayne had jumped at the opportunity.

"I think she's getting hungry."

"We'll be at the house in another few minutes. Sorry for the long ride, but I wanted to make sure we weren't followed. I made a thirty-minute trip into a two-hour journey."

"I should be the one to apologize for dragging you out on a night like this."

"You didn't drag me. Chance did, and I don't mind. He's right to be concerned. Neither of us wanted you standing around waiting while he got his mother settled in at this place."

"I hope Lila's okay. She seemed really shaken." Rayne had been reluctant to leave her. Only the thought of what could happen to Emma if she stayed had got her moving away from Lila and into Kane's SUV. She had to keep her daughter safe. Had to do whatever it took to protect her from whomever had thrown the bomb.

"She'll be fine. She's a strong lady."

"I know she is. I just wish…"

"That none of this had happened?"

"Yes."

"Don't. All this, everything that's happened, it's for a reason. You may not see it now, but you will eventually."

"Skylar said you were a smart guy."

"Yeah? Well, she told *me* that if anything happened to you, she'd hold me personally responsible."

"She did?"

"She said a few other things, but I'm trying to forget them. Something about hanging me up by my toes and quitting her job to work for the competition." He sounded amused, and Rayne could almost hear Skylar's voice, her New York accent rich and colorful as she explained exactly what she intended to do.

"Was that before I left Arizona?"

"That was this afternoon. She called to ask when Information Unlimited was going to find Darren Leon. She thinks things are taking too long and demanded that I put a few more men on the case."

"I'm so sorry, Kane."

"No need to apologize. Skylar and I have a long history, and I wouldn't have expected anything less from her. As a matter of fact, I'd have been disappointed if she hadn't called to give me grief."

Rayne could think of a few things besides disappointment that she'd have felt.

Relief, for one.

Not that she was surprised by Skylar's actions.

Like Rayne's brother, Jonas, Skylar believed in taking action. She didn't sit back, didn't wait, didn't allow others to control her life or her destiny. There'd been plenty of times since they'd met that Rayne wished she was more like her sister-in-law. As a matter of fact, Skylar had been the inspiration for rule number one.

The rule Rayne had broken a dozen times in the past twenty-four hours.

Which was why she was sitting in an SUV, being driven to a house out in the middle of nowhere.

Chance had called Kane.

They'd made the decision.

Rayne had gone along with it, letting herself rely on them to keep her and Emma safe.

It was the smart thing to do, of course.

The thing that made the most sense.

Still, she couldn't help thinking that Skylar would have done something else. Maybe climbed a mountain bare-handed and hidden in a cave until things cooled down.

"Your brother called, too. I'm happy to report that he was much more civilized. No graphic threats, just a reminder that he was trusting me with his only sister and that I'd better not let him down."

"Wonderful." Things just kept getting better and better.

"It's good to have family who care."

"I know. I just don't want them to fly up here because they think they can solve my problems for me."

"There are worse things in life than having family trying to take care of you."

"That's not what it's about, Kane. I'm twenty-eight. I've been independent for a long time, and my family needs to see that I can take care of myself. Besides, I'm worried about Skylar. I don't want her to put herself in danger because of me."

"She survived six days alone in the desert. I think she can take care of herself."

"I know, but she has more to worry about than herself now."

"Your brother is tough, too. He can hold his own against a guy like Leon blindfolded."

"That's not what I meant, either. After what happened to my brother's first wife and son, I don't want Skylar to take any unnecessary risks while she's pregnant."

"Skylar? Pregnant?"

"She didn't tell you?"

"Not yet. She's probably afraid I'll cut down on her workload when I find out. I think she and I are going to have a long talk tomorrow."

"How about you wait until she tells you the news herself?"

"So you can avoid taking the heat for revealing something she wasn't ready to share?"

"Something like that."

"I'll tell you what. I'll keep quiet if you agree to stay in the safe house until Chance and I decide it's safe for you to leave."

"That's blackmail."

"I'm well aware of that."

"Yet you sound as if you don't feel the least bit guilty about it."

"Why should I when it's for a good cause? As long as you stay concealed, you'll be safe, Emma will be safe and a woman I love like a sister won't feel compelled to fly into danger to protect either of you."

"When you put it that way, I guess I can see your point."

"Good. Lord willing, you and I will be working together for a long time. I'd hate for there to be hard feelings between us."

"You mean, I'm still going to have a job after this is over?"

"Why wouldn't you?"

"Because I may not be able to work until Leon is found, and I haven't accrued much personal leave."

"You *won't* be able to work until then, but that isn't a reason for you to lose your job. As I said, my employees are like family. I take care of them. Here we are. Your home for the foreseeable future." He turned onto a snow-covered road, pulled up in front of a two-story bungalow. Lights were blazing in the lower level, and a shadow moved in front of a window.

"Someone is in there."

"Sydney Linden. She owns the house. She and my wife are friends. Syd used to be a sniper with the Seattle Police Department."

"I didn't realize I'd be staying with some-one."

"I must have forgotten to mention it."

"Forgot or decided not to?"

"Does it matter?"

"I guess not. I'm here now, and Emma is about ready to start howling. Staying with a stranger seems preferable to sitting in this car for another few hours with a screaming baby." She unbuckled Emma, lifted her from the car seat and got out of the SUV, her eyes drawn to another vehicle in the driveway.

Another SUV.

One she recognized.

One she'd ridden in several times.

One that belonged to someone she had definitely *not* planned to see at the safe house.

"Is there something else you decided not to mention?" she asked.

"Would my mentioning that Chance was going to be staying here with you have changed anything?"

Probably not.

For sure, not.

But knowing would have helped her prepare her fickle, foolish heart. Instead, butterflies danced in her stomach and her heart did a happy little jig. All because she was going to see Chance again.

Stupid heart. When would it learn?

The door opened before they reached it, and a pretty red-haired woman motioned for them to come in. Pale, with deep circles beneath her eyes, she looked tired, her smile just shy of sincere. "Come on in."

"Sorry for barging in on you like this, Sydney."

"No, you're not, but if I didn't want you here, I would have said so."

"Thanks. I think. This is Rayne Sampson, and the baby is her daughter, Emma."

"The upstairs guest room is ready for both of you. The bed is just a futon, but there's a crib for the baby. My friends from Seattle use it when they come to visit with their son. Worked out well for you and Emma that I had it."

"Thanks for putting us up on such short notice. I know it's an inconvenience," Rayne responded, but her focus was on the room beyond the foyer. A large, cozy fire crackled in the fireplace, and Chance stood in the center of the room, hands in his pockets, dark hair falling over his forehead.

She'd thought for sure she'd left him behind at his mother's place. Had said goodbye as if she meant it forever.

And as quickly as she'd said it, they were back in each other's lives.

"There's no need for thanks. I've got stew on the stove. Come into the kitchen when you're ready. I'll dish it up for you." Sydney shot a hard look in Kane's direction and stalked away.

"She's not happy I'm here."

"Syd is a hermit. She prefers being alone to being with people."

"Then maybe we should leave and let her be alone."

"She's also an expert marksman, Rayne. You'll be safer here than anywhere else I can think of. Besides, as Sydney said, if she didn't want you here, you wouldn't be here."

"I still don't feel comfortable staying." Rayne frowned, juggling Emma in one arm and reaching into the diaper bag with the other.

Trying not to look as Chance walked into the foyer, trying not to drink him in as some love-lorn Victorian maid might drink in the sight of the lord of the manor.

*Love*lorn? There it was.

That word.

The one that went with rule number three.

Never, ever, ever, *ever* fall in love again.

"Sydney is as blunt as they come. If she gets tired of having you here, she'll let me know. In the meantime, don't let her intimidate you. I'll grab your overnight case from the SUV and bring it in. Then I'd better get out of here. The snow is piling up quick." He walked outside before she could think of a way to get out of spending another minute in the same house with her taciturn hostess and Chance.

Chance.

The man she'd broken rules one and two for.

The man she should not, would not, could not break rule three for.

She'd made her one big mistake in love.

She wouldn't make another one.

Never, ever, ever, ever.

"You can't avoid looking at me forever,"

he said, and she walked into the living room, pulled Emma's bottle from the diaper bag.

"I can try," she muttered, and he had the nerve to laugh. "It's not funny, Chance. You weren't supposed to be here."

"Who says?"

"Me."

"Sorry to disappoint you, but I'm here, and I'm staying for the duration." His voice was smooth as melted chocolate, his eyes light, silvery blue.

Something she wouldn't have noticed if she weren't staring straight into them.

Darn the man.

"I need to heat up Emma's bottle. She's hungry."

"Changing the subject?"

"It seemed like the easiest thing to do. We're both tired, and I'm not in the mood for verbal combat."

"Does that mean you're calling a truce?"

"For tonight? Yes."

"Good, because I'd rather fight your enemy than fight you." He studied her face, his gaze skimming along her cheeks, her jaw, her lips, staying there for a heartbeat too long.

"As I said, I need to heat up Emma's bottle." She also needed to clear her head, focus on what was important. Chance, his eyes, his velvety voice, his solid, dependable presence, didn't matter nearly as much as finding out who'd thrown a bomb at his mother's house.

Darren Leon was the obvious suspect, and the most likely person to want her dead. The *only* person to want her dead, as far as she could recall.

But something niggled at the back of her mind, a partial memory that wouldn't quite surface.

Emma.

Danger.

That's all she could grasp, and she looked down at her daughter, cold, sick dread filling her stomach, the way it had so many times since she'd woken after the accident.

"What is it?" Chance asked, and she knew she must look as shaken as she felt.

"Something... A feeling. A memory. I don't know, I can't hold on to it long enough to figure it out. I just have this sense that Emma is in danger."

"You think that is what all this is about? The

bomb? The phone call? All of it? You think someone is trying to harm Emma?"

"I don't know. I just wish I could remember. Were you able to get my laptop from the apartment? Maybe there's something on it that will spark a memory."

"Yes. Kane is going to bring it to the office tomorrow. If Sam can't access the deleted emails, no one can."

"If he can, maybe I'll finally have some answers."

"In the meantime, we'll be vigilant when it comes to Emma's protection. Though, from where I'm standing, it looks like you're the one in danger. Come on. I'll take you to the kitchen. Maybe Sydney has a bottle warmer." Chance took Emma from her arms.

"How was I acting in the days before the accident?"

"Quiet. Mom thought you were working too hard."

"She said that?"

"Yes. Right before she told me I should take you out to dinner."

"Oh."

"I'm afraid my mother is a matchmaker at heart."

"Do you think that's why she said I didn't seem like myself? Because she wanted an excuse to try to get you to ask me out? Or do you think something more was going on?"

"At the time, I didn't think much about it either way, but my mother is opportunistic. She's not a liar. I'd say she noticed something and tried to take advantage of it to throw us together. Why are you asking about how you were acting? More memories and feelings?"

"Unfortunately, no. I just wonder what was going on the week before the accident. Actually, I wonder what was going on for the seven weeks before the accident."

"You worked. You went to church. You seemed like you'd settled in pretty easily."

"And did we...?" *Don't ask. Do* not *ask.*

"Go out to dinner? Neither of us were in the market for a relationship, remember?"

"Of course."

"Disappointed?" He opened a door to the left of the foyer and led her through a large dining room.

"Not at all."

"That's what I keep telling myself, too."

He opened another door, ushered her into the kitchen.

Thank goodness.

No way could they finish the conversation in front of Sydney. No way could Rayne open her mouth and make more of a fool of herself than she already had.

"Ready for that stew?" Sydney crossed the room, her bare feet padding on the wood floor, her red hair swinging with every step.

"Actually, I was hoping I could heat up Emma's bottle."

"No problem." She snagged the bottle, popped it into a stainless-steel microwave.

"Your home is lovely." *Keep her talking. Keep her in the room. Anything to avoid being alone with Chance.*

"It is, but it's not really mine."

"No?"

"It belongs to my mother-in-law. She's spending the winter in Florida, and she asked me to house-sit."

"I hope she and your husband don't mind us hanging out here for a few days," Rayne replied as Chance took the bottle from the microwave, checked the temperature of the formula, offered it to Emma as if he'd done it a hundred times before.

"My mother-in-law will be fine with it. My husband was killed in Iraq five years ago."

"I'm so sorry." Rayne's heart went out to Sydney. She couldn't imagine being widowed at such a young age.

"That's what everyone says," said Sydney, as she pulled two bowls from a cupboard, ladled stew into both and set them down on a small kitchen table. Stiff-shouldered, blank-faced, definitely not in the mood to keep talking about her husband.

"Anyone here?" Kane called from the living room, cutting through the sudden tension in the room.

"In the kitchen. You want stew?" Sydney responded, grabbing another bowl as Kane opened the kitchen door.

"No. I need to get going." Snow flecked his brown hair, and he brushed it off. "Your bag is out in the living room, Rayne. I'll let Chance take it to your room. If you need anything, give me a call."

"You've already done more than enough. I don't know how I'll ever thank you."

"You'll thank me by staying here until it's safe to leave."

"Where would I go? We're in the middle of nowhere and I don't have a car."

"I don't know, but if you're anything like Skylar, you'll find some way to get into trouble."

"I wish I were like her, but I'm not, so I'll stay."

"Glad to hear it. Chance, this case is officially on your docket. Let me know if you need someone to take over any of your other cases."

"I should be fine. I've just closed three of the five you assigned me."

"Wait a minute. I'm *not* a case, and I don't need to be assigned to anybody."

"I'll check in tomorrow morning." Kane ignored Rayne's protest, offered a quick wave and let the door swing shut again.

"He knows how to stage a fast retreat," Sydney noted wryly as she handed Rayne a spoon.

"Kane is nothing if not quick," said Chance, who settled into a chair, as Emma ate greedily, her eyes drooping as she stared up into his face. She looked comfortable, content, safe. All the things Rayne wanted for her. Her throat tightened at the thought, the dreams she'd once had wrapped up in that picture. A cozy kitchen, a caring man, a baby or two or three.

Three.

Remember rule three.

Never, ever, ever, ever fall in love again.

Ever.

Even if the person you're falling for is someone like Chance.

She needed to tack the last thought onto the end, or she might start to think there were exceptions to the rule.

One exception.

An exception who met her gaze, smiled into her eyes.

She scooped up a mouthful of stew, made a show of fishing out just the right piece of potato. "This is wonderful, Sydney. Thank you."

"You're welcome to seconds, thirds, fourths. Whatever you can eat."

"This will be plenty."

"The kitchen is open if you change your

mind later. I don't want to be a poor hostess, but I have a tight work schedule, and I'm behind. So if you'll excuse me, I'll leave the two of you to your meal. Rayne, your room is at the top of the stairs, first door on the left. There's an en suite bathroom. No television, but there's a radio if you want to use it. Chance, you're going to have to bunk on the pullout sofa down here. My mother-in-law would die a thousand deaths if she thought she had an unmarried couple sleeping next door to each other. There's a shower upstairs. Second door to the right. Linen closet is next to it. Help yourself to whatever you need. Good night." She disappeared into the room off the kitchen, closed the door. The soft click of the lock echoed in the silence.

TEN

Obviously, Sydney really didn't care about being a poor hostess, and obviously, she was happy to say goodnight.

Maybe it was time for Rayne and Emma to go to bed, too, because eating stew across the table from Chance did not seem like something a woman who didn't want to fall for a guy would do.

"I think I'm about done," Rayne said, carrying her half-eaten stew to the trash can and dumping it in.

"You don't have to be scared, Rayne. I'm not going to ask for something you don't want to give." Chance finished feeding Emma, lifted her to his shoulder and patted her back.

"I'm not scared."

"Then why are you running away from me?"

"I'm not. It's been a long day. Em and I are exhausted, and it's past time for us to be in bed."

"If that's the way you want to play it, I guess I'll go along with it."

"The only thing you're going along with is the truth." She *was* tired. It *was* past time for Emma to be in bed.

And she *was* running.

From him.

From herself.

She took Emma, inhaled formula and baby lotion. She and Emma were okay on their own. Had been okay for eight months. She had to keep that in mind or she might start thinking they needed something more. Might start dreaming about something more.

Some*one* more.

"I'll get your overnight case and bring it upstairs."

"I can—"

"I thought you'd called a truce for tonight."

"I did."

"So let's not waste time arguing about this. You carry Emma. I'll get the bag."

"Fine." Anything to keep things moving along, get up to the bedroom and lock herself away from Chance.

"I've been thinking. Earlier today, you told me your trouble started when Chandra died," he said as he led the way into the living room.

"It seemed that way."

"How did she die?"

"A drug overdose."

"She was an addict?"

"She had been. She got caught with cocaine during a drug raid a few years back and went to rehab. After that, I thought she was clean, but she must have fallen off the wagon."

"How long had you known her?"

"We met in kindergarten and were best friends from that day on. I loved her like a sister, Chance. I wanted to believe she'd gotten past her addiction. When she got pregnant with Emma, she was so excited. She committed to living healthy. No drugs. No alcohol. Only organic foods. Nothing that might hurt the baby."

"So what happened?"

"I still don't know. I'd never seen her as

happy as she was that month after Emma was born, and I still can't believe she OD'd."

"What did she take?"

"Prescription painkillers. Something she got after Emma was born. The empty bottle was on the table by her bed. I...saw it when I found her." She'd never forget it. The bottle lying on its side. Chandra sprawled facedown on the bed, her gorgeous hair matted and tangled. Rayne hadn't wanted to believe Chandra was dead, had called an ambulance, tried CPR, done everything she could to bring her back.

None of it had been enough.

"That must have been hard."

"It was. She had a job interview, and she asked me to take care of Emma so she could go. I'd taken off from work, spent the day enjoying playing mommy. I didn't even think about Chandra until she was an hour late picking Emma up."

"That doesn't make her death your fault. You know that, right?"

"Head knowledge and heart knowledge are two different things."

"They need to be reconciled, Rayne, if you're ever going to heal."

"That's what Michael kept telling me. He said I was taking Emma out of guilt. That I needed to reconcile my guilt with the reality of the situation and accept that I had no business being a mother and only wanted Chandra's baby because I wanted to keep a part of her alive in my life."

"I'm not sure I like being compared to Michael." He grabbed the overnight case but didn't head for the stairs. Just stood near the fireplace, light dancing across his face.

"Trust me. You're nothing like Michael."

"Should I be insulted or flattered?"

"Neither. I'm just stating a fact. Michael was a psychiatrist. Every other word out of his mouth was a question, and he picked apart every emotion he felt." Every emotion she felt, too, but that wasn't something she wanted to share.

"A psychiatrist, huh?"

"There's no need to say it like that."

"Like what?" he asked, but his smirk said he knew exactly what she meant.

"Like psychiatrists are boring, elitist snobs."

"I have a couple good friends who are in the field. That hadn't even occurred to me."

"Then what are you thinking?"

"That I can't imagine you with a guy who wanted to talk about his feelings all the time."

"Well, I *was* with a guy who wanted to talk about his feelings, so you can readjust your imaginings."

"So you were engaged to a psychiatrist who insisted you only wanted Emma because you felt guilty about her mother's death? Sounds like he was trying to manipulate you into doing what he wanted."

"Michael was a master manipulator."

"What did you see in the guy?"

Good question. One she wasn't sure she had an answer to. Though, if he'd asked her a year ago, she probably would have waxed poetic about Michael's myriad charms.

"We met when I picked Chandra up from a group therapy session. He volunteered as a counselor, and he seemed so…caring. A few weeks later, we ran into each other again at the women's shelter where I was doing my practical study for my social work degree. We started talking and I found out we attended the same church but went to different services. It seemed as if we had a lot in common."

"Or as if he worked it out so you would *think* you had a lot in common."

"What are you talking about?"

"How do you know he didn't do a little fishing, maybe ask Chandra where you worked, how you spent your time?"

"Why would he? I'm not such a great catch that a guy like Michael would work overtime to get my attention."

"I don't know. You seem like a pretty great catch to me. It isn't that big of a stretch to think that a guy you described as a master manipulator would go out of his way to manipulate you into his life." He frowned, and she had a flash of memory, a moment of clarity. Emma shrieking as Rayne stepped into a conference room, looked into gray-blue eyes, felt something spring to life.

"We met at an office, didn't we?"

"That's right. Kane wanted to introduce you to the team since you'd be working with a lot of our clients."

"The babysitter he'd set up for me canceled, and I was running late. Emma was screaming her head off, and I walked into the room and…" Saw you standing near the window and didn't notice anyone else.

"What?"

"You were standing near the window, and you didn't look happy."

"I'm not good at waiting."

"I remember that and then, nothing."

"Remembering something is a start. Be happy with it."

"I'm trying, but I'm not good at waiting, either." Especially when waiting for her memories might mean more time in Sydney's house with Chance. "I really need to get Emma to bed."

"Do you know who her father is? You've mentioned Chandra a lot, but what about Emma's birth father? She didn't just come into existence without one."

"Chandra wouldn't say. She implied that there was more than one possibility, and she left the father's name off the birth certificate."

"She implied?"

"Chandra was…Chandra. I loved her, but she lived by her own rules. They weren't rules I understood."

"Then how did you stay friends for so long?"

"When she cared, Chandra cared deeply. She supported my goals and dreams. She wanted the best for me. Despite her faults, she was a generous and loving person."

"I wish I could have met her."

"I wish you could have, too." She blinked back tears and walked up the stairs, her heart thudding with grief for what Chandra could have been, the life she could have lived with Emma.

"What did she think of Michael?" Chance followed her up and carried the overnight case into a cozy guest room.

"They weren't best friends, but they got along."

"But what did she *think* of him? You were best friends, right? Surely, she had something to say about him."

"Not really. I think it was a little awkward, me dating the guy who ran her group counseling sessions. She didn't like to talk about him. She went with it, though, because she knew it made me happy."

"So she tolerated him?"

"I didn't say that, and you're asking an awful lot of questions. If I didn't know better I'd think you were…" She met his eyes. "You *are* inter-rogating me!"

"Interviewing. That's a lot more friendly." He didn't even have the decency to look sorry.

"Well, your interview is going to have to end. Emma is sleeping, and I plan to join her the minute you leave the room."

"You sound angry."

"And you sound like Michael."

"That was a low blow, Goldilocks." He scowled.

He was right.

Low.

Uncalled for.

Unnecessary.

"I'm sorry. You're trying to help. I know that. I just don't like being manipulated. After three years of it, I'm done."

"Apology accepted. But, just so we're clear, I was interviewing you. Plain and simple. Kane assigned your case to me. I take that seriously. If I had been trying to manipulate you, you never would have known it. I'll be downstairs if you need anything." He stepped out of the room and closed the door, leaving Rayne to think about what he'd said.

What she'd said.

How foolish and silly she'd been to even think that Chance would stoop so low.

He wasn't that kind of guy, and if she had any kind of courage in her at all, she'd march back down the stairs and tell him as much.

But she didn't.

When it came to matters of the heart, she was as big a coward as they came.

Heart?

No way.

Just friendship, and hurting a friend was never the right thing to do.

She changed Emma, tucked her into the crib, prayed for her. When she finished, she wanted to take a shower, pull on her comfortable flannel pajamas and curl up on the futon.

She couldn't.

Her parents had raised her to face her mistakes head-on, and if she were going to get any sleep, she was going to have to face this one.

She took a deep breath, splashed cold water on her hot face, trying not to look too long at her bruised cheek and lumpy head, her shadow-rimmed eyes or her pale skin.

None of those things mattered.

What mattered was saying what needed to be said.

She took a deep breath, opened the door and walked straight into Chance's arms.

Surprised, she stumbled back, nearly falling.

"Careful." His hands were on her waist, his palms warm, and she forgot everything she was supposed to say.

"I thought you were downstairs," she managed, and he raised a dark eyebrow.

"I was heading to the shower. Where were you heading?"

"To see you."

"Did you need something?"

"Just to apologize."

"You already did."

"I said I was sorry, but what I should have said was that I know you would never manipulate me. I know you're not that kind of person, and I don't know why I said what I did."

"You don't have to explain."

"Yes. I do. You've been nothing but kind and helpful. I couldn't ask for a better friend in adversity, and I really am sorry."

He studied her for a moment, and then he leaned so close they were almost nose to nose.

"You're making me sound like a saint, and I can guarantee you I'm not. I'm telling you right now that it's not just friendship I have on my mind when I'm with you. So how about we talk about this tomorrow when we're both in better frames of mind?" His hands dropped, and he walked into the room across the hall, closed the door, left her standing with her mouth hanging open.

It's not just friendship I have on my mind when I'm with you?

Well, it wasn't friendship she had on her mind, either.

Which was unfortunate, seeing as how she was *not* going to break the last rule.

Ever.

No exceptions.

Definitely.

Probably.

Hopefully?

She stepped back in the room, closed the door and grabbed her flannel PJs, praying that when morning came, she'd wake up and realize that everything she'd lived through in the past twenty-four hours had been a dream.

ELEVEN

Mornings were supposed to bring fresh perspective, right?

So why didn't Chance have any?

He scowled at the computer screen, rereading Sam Goodwin's email. Kane had dropped Rayne's computer off with Sam the previous night, and he'd already examined it. His verdict: it had been cleaned.

Which begged the question: Who had done the cleaning?

Rayne?

Someone else?

If someone else, then why? When? How?

He poured a cup of coffee from the pot he'd made an hour before, set it on the kitchen table next to the computer. He might not have fresh perspective, but at least a good night's sleep had given him renewed energy.

Footsteps sounded on stairs, and Chance braced himself for what he knew he'd feel when Rayne appeared. All the emotions that he'd promised himself he'd never give in to were back, stronger than they'd been with Jessica.

He couldn't explain it.

Didn't like it.

Wasn't sure what it said about the relationship he'd had with his wife. Maybe only that there'd been something missing, some vital connection that he wouldn't know existed if he hadn't met Rayne.

She walked into the kitchen, her hair pulled back in a high ponytail, her face scrubbed clean. No makeup covering the bruises, nothing to hide the circles beneath her eyes. Faded jeans and a well-worn T-shirt her only adornment, she walked with the graceful ease of a dancer.

And she took his breath away.

"You're up early," she said, her cheeks tinged

with more pink than he'd seen since the accident.

"So are you."

"Any sign of Sydney?"

"She popped out of her room about twenty minutes ago, grabbed coffee and went back in."

"She's very private."

"It seems that way. Where's Emma?"

"Still sound asleep. She woke a few times last night, so I'm not surprised. Poor baby. She really needs her routine back."

"She'll get it."

"Eventually, but that could mean days or weeks or longer. I'm not sure how she's going to handle that."

"How about you? How will you handle it if this stretches out for weeks?"

"I'll manage." She offered a brittle smile. "What are you working on?"

"Going over a few emails. The computer whiz I told you about checked your computer. He said it's been cleaned."

"Like what you do if your computer has a virus?"

"Exactly. It's been cleaned and rebuilt. Looks

like it happened the day of your accident. Is it something you might have done?"

"I've done it a couple of times. My father taught me how when I was in college after my computer was infected with a virus."

"So it's within the realm of possibility that you cleaned and rebuilt it yourself?"

"Who else would? No one uses my computer except me."

"Maybe someone who was concerned with what might be on your computer and decided to make sure whatever was there disappeared for good."

"Who? I only communicate with friends and coworkers. And what good would it do to get rid of my emails? No one could have known I'd get amnesia. I should have been able to re-member what the emails said whether I'd kept them or not."

"That leaves one possibility." He eyed her over the rim of his coffee cup, watching as his meaning sank in.

"You think my accident wasn't an accident at all, and someone wanted to kill me? Someone I'd been in contact with, who could be traced through my emails? Impossible. None of my friends would want to harm me, and my co-workers are all people you know. Do you really believe any of them would bomb your mother's house?"

"It's not what either of us believes that matters. It's the facts."

"Well, the facts are that I have great friends. None of them would do this. Leon is our only suspect. If the police can find him, maybe we'll get some answers."

"Leon was the first person I thought of, but how could he have found you? Your number is unlisted. I tried calling information to get your address. No dice. Leon couldn't be the one who called you out to the airport. Even if he had your number, you're not friends—you wouldn't have gone to pick him up."

"What I told you still holds true. Aside from Leon, there isn't anyone who would want to hurt me."

"How about Emma's father?" It was a possibility he'd been thinking about most of the morning. One that might not make sense, but that he couldn't shake.

"I don't know who he is, and he doesn't know me. As a matter of fact, he doesn't even know

Emma exists. Chandra told me that she never informed the father about her pregnancy."

"Was Chandra always honest with you?"

"For the most part."

"Which means she could have lied."

"She could have, but what would her motive have been? Whether or not she informed the father was her business. As much as I wanted her do the right thing, I couldn't make her and she knew it."

"I guess we'll need to dig a little deeper to find out who she told."

"Right now, all I want to dig into is the refrigerator." She opened the stainless-steel refrigerator and stared into the brightly lit interior. "Want some eggs?"

"Are you cooking?"

"Since you're working, yes."

"That sounds very…" He almost said *domestic,* but if he used the word, she'd probably run. "Good."

"That's not you were really going to say, is it?" she asked as she cracked eggs into a bowl and dug a pan out of a cupboard.

"Not exactly."

"So maybe I'm not the only chicken around here."

"It's not me who'd be scared of what I almost said."

"Then say it."

"I was going to say, your making eggs for both of us seems very domestic."

If he hadn't been watching so intently, he would have missed the tiny hitch in her movements as she shoved bread into the toaster. "Everything a person does in a kitchen seems domestic."

"Not if it's being done alone. Add another person, then things get interesting."

"I still think Leon is our guy," she said, changing the subject without apology.

"He's an easy scapegoat, anyway." But it seemed to Chance that if a guy like Leon wanted revenge, he could have gotten it more easily the day he'd held Rayne at gunpoint. Load the gun, pull the trigger, finish it right there and then.

Why stretch things out? Why wait until Rayne moved away?

"You said you'd helped Leon's wife start fresh. What happened to her?"

"As far as I know, she's still in Baltimore enjoying the job I found for her."

"Do you have her contact information?"

"Yes, but I can't imagine that she has anything to do with any of this."

"How about you let me check it out anyway? It can't hurt to know for sure."

"It's on my…"

"Computer?"

"Yes. So, I guess I don't have it after all."

"You know her name and her employer, right?"

"Her name is Mary Harper. She works for All His Children preschool."

"That should be enough to find her."

"Thanks, but I don't know if it will do any good. It seems as if we're just grasping at straws, hoping we'll find something." She set a plate of eggs and toast in front of him, took the seat across the table.

"They might be straws, but at least we have something to grasp. That's a lot more than I have with some cases."

She shrugged, probably not convinced.

He didn't blame her.

It seemed they had a lot more questions than

they had answers, but he wouldn't give up. He'd keep searching, keep grasping until he finally pulled up something that would lead them in the right direction.

"I wonder how your mother is doing this morning," Rayne said.

"I spoke to her a half hour ago. She's doing okay."

"I'm glad. Despite what you both say, I still feel bad about what happened."

"Don't waste your energy feeling bad, okay? My mother specifically told me to tell you that."

"Your mother is kind to worry about me when her house just burned to the ground."

"The damage isn't nearly as bad as it looked. The fire marshal already cleared it for cleaning and rebuilding. The structure is still sound. It's just the front facade that will have to be replaced. The porch is gone, but the things that are important are still intact."

"That's a relief. I've been worried that the entire house would have to be torn down." She stabbed a bite of egg, and Chance reached for her hand.

"Since we're sitting here being domestic, we might as well go a step further."

Her eyes widened, her gaze dropping to his lips, and everything he'd been thinking slipped away until there was nothing but the two of them, hands touching, eyes meeting, the thing that had been pulling them together, drawing them even closer.

"That's probably not a good idea." But she didn't sound as convinced as he thought she would, and he didn't feel nearly as convinced as he knew he should.

No more relationships.

That had been the plan for years.

Suddenly, the plan was changing, all the things he'd thought were true called into question by a woman he'd spent weeks avoiding and two days protecting.

"I meant, how about we pray together before we eat? Of course, after that, I'm not opposed to whatever else you had in mind."

Heat shot up Rayne's neck, and she dropped her gaze. "Let's pray."

He took a deep breath, steadying himself as he asked God's blessing on the food. The silent prayer he added as Rayne prayed was between him and God, but he hoped he'd have an answer soon. Clarity in the face of confusion. Vision in the face of darkness. Patience in the face of what might turn out to be the toughest investigation he'd ever conducted. He needed all those things, and he needed them yesterday.

"Amen," Rayne mumbled, her neck and cheeks still stained pink.

"There's no need to be embarrassed."

"I'm not."

"Then why are you three shades of red?"

"Because I'm overheated from standing beside a hot stove."

"You were cooking eggs. How hot did the stove need to be?"

"Hot?"

"You're a bad liar, you know that?" He stood, pulling her up with one gentle tug of the hand.

"I'm not lying."

"No?"

"I'm just not telling the entire truth." She offered a quick smile, her dimple there and gone in a flash, and he leaned close, inhaled soap and subtle perfume.

"So what *is* the truth, Goldilocks?" He

twirled a curl around his finger, straightened it, watched as it sprang back.

"All the things I feel when I'm with you terrify me, but when I'm with you, I'm drawn to you like a moth to the flame. I can't resist."

"Should I be upset about that?" Chance asked.

"Of course not. When I'm incinerated, you'll be just fine."

"The way I see it, we're both moths drawn to the same flame. Only time will tell if we'll survive."

"I don't want a relationship, Chance."

"I know."

"And you don't want one, either."

"I know that, too."

"So what are we doing?"

"We're realizing that sometimes the things we don't want are the things that God gives us, and we're trying to figure out what to do with that."

Emma's cry drifted from upstairs and Rayne pulled away. Nearly *ran* away.

Chance let her go.

There was nothing he could say that could change what was.

They'd both hurt and been hurt. They'd both failed in love. And now they were together, drawn by something neither of them could understand.

His phone rang, and he answered it, glad for the distraction.

"Hello?"

"Chance? It's Kai. I have some information I thought you'd want."

"Go ahead."

"Looks like the bomb was fairly rudimentary. Anyone with a little ingenuity could have made it."

"Not helpful."

"No, but there is something that might be. That truck you saw? It's a rental."

"How do you figure that?"

"A little footwork. I went to the airport, checked with car-rental companies. One of them rented a dark blue Mitsubishi truck to a guy named Daryl Green the day before yesterday. Funny thing is, I saw a copy of Green's photo ID, and he looks a lot like Darren Leon. Lighter hair and clean-shaven, but they could be the same guy."

"Could be or are?"

"I'm ninety percent sure it's him, but we're having an expert compare the ID photo with Leon's mug shot. In the meantime, we're checking local hotels to see if Green checked in."

"Seems like that would make things a little too easy."

"I'm all for things being easy. I have a report to type up. I'll call you if we locate Green." Kai hung up, and Chance shoved the phone back in his pocket.

"Bad news?" Rayne carried Emma into the kitchen, and the baby reached for him, her chubby hands grasping at air, and he couldn't seem to resist her anymore than he could resist her mother. He took her from Rayne, tickled her belly while he explained what he'd learned.

"So he *is* after me," she said, when he finished, her eyes wide with fear.

"It looks that way."

"I know I said he was the only one I could think of, but..."

"What?"

"It doesn't make sense. You're right that I'd never have gone to the airport to meet him."

"But you did go to the airport."

"I know." She shoved hair behind her ear, the gesture impatient and quick.

"We'll figure it out."

"You always say that," she grumbled, setting Emma in a high chair that stood in a corner of the room.

"I always mean it."

"Well, I'm glad one of us has confidence."

"Come here." He tugged her into his chest, and she sighed, her arms sliding around his waist, her hands resting on his back. She fit perfectly there.

"Am I interrupting something?" Sydney walked into the room, and Rayne jumped back, tripping over the high chair in her haste.

"Slow down, Rayne. Hugging me isn't a crime." He grabbed her arm before she could face plant.

"You're not interrupting," she responded to Sydney's question, ignoring his comment as she pulled a small box of Cheerios from the diaper bag.

"You're not going to feed her that for breakfast, are you?" Sydney asked.

"I forgot to pack her cereal and fruit."

"I have plenty of baby stuff in the basement

pantry. Come on. I'll show you where it is. You want to leave Emma here or take her?"

"I…" She met Chance's eyes.

"She'll be fine here."

"Are you sure?"

"We haven't had any trouble getting along yet, have we, kid?" He chucked Emma under the chin and she grinned.

"All right. As long as you're sure," Rayne said as she followed Sydney out of the room. Emma started fussing almost immediately, her big blue eyes welling with tears.

"Don't do that, kid." He pulled her out of the high chair, carried her to the window.

Outside, the wind howled, bending towering pine trees and sending snowdrifts up the side of the wood fence that surrounded the yard. Not a good day to be outside, but an easy day to stay safe. Unless Leon was desperate, he wouldn't be driving the roads, trolling for his victim.

Emma patted his cheek, demanding his attention. He looked down into her chubby face and caught a glimpse of a future he hadn't thought he'd wanted but knew he couldn't turn away from.

Whatever it took, he'd protect Rayne and

Emma, and when it was over, there'd be no walking away.

He'd changed in the past couple of days.

He couldn't regret it. All he could do was step forward in faith and see where God would lead him.

TWELVE

Three days stuck in a house with a stranger, a fussy baby and a man she desperately needed to avoid wasn't high on the list of things Rayne wanted to do with her life.

She'd done it anyway.

Spent three days tiptoeing around Sydney's place, eating meals at the kitchen table, Emma squirming and fussing in her lap, Chance across the table, talking and smiling and acting like they were a happy little family.

Only they weren't a family, and Rayne wasn't happy.

At least she shouldn't be. Somehow, though, sitting with Chance, listening to him talk about his work, his life, his dreams, felt right. No doubt about it, the longer she spent stuck in the house with him, the more likely she was to do the unthinkable.

Break rule number three.

Fall.

Hard.

Unfortunately, despite the best efforts of the Spokane Sheriff's Department, Leon was still on the loose. Despite Rayne's best efforts to remember the night of the accident, her mind was empty of anything but vague, shadowy images. Darkness. Light. Fear. Nothing she could hang on to.

Which was why she'd be spending another day tiptoeing around Sydney's house, trying not to be in the way, trying to stay out of Chance's way, trying not to feel as if she was a prisoner of circumstances and of her own fickle emotions.

She glanced at the glowing numbers on the clock that sat on a table near the futon. A few more hours and the sun would be up. Day four with little hope of it being the last day of her sentence.

She frowned.

Not a sentence.

A safety precaution.

That's what her brother, Jonas, had said when she'd called and told him where she was, who she was with, why.

Stay put.

Do what Chance and Kane tell you.

She could hear the words as clearly as if he were standing in the room saying them. She wanted to shrug them off, but not nearly as much as she wanted to stay alive. Not that she was afraid to die. She wasn't. She was afraid to leave Emma motherless. Jonas and Skylar had agreed to be Emma's guardians if something happened to Rayne, but Rayne wanted to be around as Emma grew, wanted to walk her to school on the first day of kindergarten, take her to ballet lessons, teach her to tie her shoes.

She paced across the room, wishing she could turn on the radio, but afraid the noise would wake Emma. It had taken nearly an hour for the baby to fall asleep. The last thing Rayne wanted was for her to wake up. Maybe she could sneak down to the kitchen for a snack instead. There'd been a bag of mini-chocolate bars in one of the cupboards. That sounded like the perfect prescription for stress reduction.

She crept down the stairs and through the dining room. No way would she walk through the living room where Chance slept. No lights, but she didn't need them to scout out a bag of chocolate. She opened one cupboard, then another, scowling when she came up empty.

There *had* been a bag of chocolate bars—she was certain of it.

"Looking for something?" Chance's voice cut through the darkness and she jumped, whirling around to face him.

"What are you doing up?" she whispered, her heart pounding double time.

"I was going to ask you the same thing." He flipped on a light over the stove, the golden glow highlighting the angles and planes of his face.

Gorgeous.

No other way to say it.

No way to deny it.

She looked away, looked back, trying not to ogle. Really, really trying. "I came down for some chocolate."

"One of those nights, huh?" He didn't seem nearly as uncomfortable as she was.

And why should he be?

Why should *she* be?

She had a father and a brother and had run into them around the house at all hours. There was nothing special about a late night chat… in a dimly lit room…with a very appealing man…

Yet Chance was…

Different.

It wasn't just his looks that made him seem that way, wasn't even *mostly* his looks. It was his attitude, his faith, his spirit of service.

His impressive biceps didn't hurt, either.

He reached into a cupboard above the sink and pulled out a bag of miniature candy bars. "There you go. An entire bag of chocolate. Now how about we sit down and you tell me why you're up at three in the morning?" He tugged open the bag of chocolates and ate one.

"Hey!"

"There are plenty more, Goldilocks."

"I really wish you'd stop calling me that."

"Okay."

"And while you're at it, you can stop being so easy to get along with."

"I'll do my best."

She scowled and he chuckled, unwrapping

another chocolate and handing it to her. "So spill. What's got you growling this morning?"

"This house. Leon. You. Me. Everything." She popped the chocolate into her mouth and reached for another one.

"And you think chocolate is going to help?"

"It can't hurt."

"I have a better idea."

"No."

"You haven't even heard what it is," Chance said with an impish grin.

"I don't need to. If it involves spending time with you, it's a very, very bad idea."

"Why's that?"

"Have you forgotten rule number three, Chance? The only rule I've yet to break. The one rule I'm not going to break. Not even for you."

"You never did tell me what that rule was."

"And I'm never going to."

"Okay, but since you're not going to break it, you've got nothing to worry about. Come on. Let me show you what I had in mind." He pulled her to her feet, grabbing the bag of chocolate bars as he walked across the room.

"I really don't think this is a good idea,"

Rayne said, but she walked with him anyway. Through the dining room, into the foyer and then into the living room. Firelight illuminated the room, reflecting off the cover of Chance's laptop.

"Were you working?"

"I have a couple of cases I'm finishing up." He pulled a blanket from the back of the couch, spread it on the floor.

"At three in the morning?"

"You're not the only one who has things on their mind."

"I'm sorry. I should have asked before now. What's bothering you enough to keep you awake at this time of the morning?"

"Nothing a few minutes watching the fire burn won't solve."

"I don't think watching a fire—"

"That's your problem, Rayne. You think too much." He sat and tugged her down beside him, opened up a candy bar and handed it to her.

Firelight played across her face, warming tense muscles, relaxing her in a way she hadn't expected.

He handed her another chocolate, but she passed it back.

"Thanks. I've had enough."

"Since when are three mini-chocolate bars enough for anyone?" Chance asked, popping the chocolate into his mouth, his silvery gaze trailing over her face.

"Since I stopped growing up and started growing out."

"I'm surprised." He raised an eyebrow and she frowned.

"By what?"

"The fact that you count calories. You're too thin by a lot of people's standards. As a matter of fact, in many cultures, you'd need to fatten up if you ever wanted to receive a marriage proposal."

"I wouldn't ever want another one, so I guess it's not something I need to worry about."

"That's not the point. The point is, you're perfect the way you are, so why deny yourself something you love for the sake of someone else's ideal?"

"I'm not denying myself anything." Or maybe she was. Three years of watching Michael carefully portion everything he ate, three years of him reminding her that she couldn't afford to gain any more weight, three years of looking in the mirror and seeing her curves as a burden, and every bite of something she loved had become a danger zone she needed to be wary of.

She scowled. "I thought you said sitting here was going to help."

"It will. Just give it time." He unwrapped another chocolate, pressed it to her lips, and she had no choice but to eat it.

"Chance—"

"If you don't let yourself relax, the fire won't work."

"I can't relax. There's too much going on. Or not enough going on. I don't know which." She paced to the window, looked out into the darkness. Bright moonlight spilled onto crisp white snowdrifts, illuminating the landscape. Pine boughs undulated rhythmically, the wind blowing snow and ice from their branches.

"There's a lot of work going on, Rayne. We'll have our answers eventually."

"I know, and I appreciate everything everyone is doing, but this isn't what I thought my life would be like when I moved to Spokane."

"What did you think it would be like?"

"Peaceful. Fresh. New. Instead, it's exactly what it was those last few months in Arizona. I keep feeling as if there's a reason for it. Like maybe God is trying to teach me to rely on Him or maybe He's trying to show me that I've made a wrong turn in my life, but no matter how much I try to figure it out, I'm just not sure what He's saying."

"It's tough when you don't feel as if there's clear direction."

"It's also tough to hear myself whining. I'm not usually like this." She tried to laugh, but the sound fell flat.

"You're not whining. Much."

This time she really did laugh. "At least you're honest."

"This will all be over soon. You'll be able to go back to your life, go back to looking for whatever it is you were hoping you'd find when you moved here."

"I wasn't looking for anything. I was starting fresh."

"We're all looking for something, Rayne. For some of us, that means running away from everything we've ever known. For others, it

means running back to what we left behind."
Chance moved up behind her, not touching but
close enough that his breath ruffled her hair,
his warmth seeped through her flannel pajamas.

Pajamas?

She glanced down at the neon green frogs
and bright pink hearts that danced across sky-
blue fabric.

Perfect.

"They're cute."

"What?"

"The pajamas."

"Thanks."

He chuckled, and she truly relaxed for the
first time in way too many hours. "Would you
rather I'd said they were beautiful?"

"I'd rather you'd not have seen me in them at
all."

"You came downstairs, Rayne. Didn't you
think I'd hear you and come to see what was
wrong?"

"I had chocolate on the brain. I wasn't thinking about much of anything." But she should
have known he'd come. That's the way Chance
was. Always there when she needed him.

Not that she needed him.

She didn't need anyone but God, Emma and herself.

The thought clogged her throat, filled her eyes.

But she was *not* going to cry.

No way in the world would she let Chance see her wearing her froggy flannel, tears dripping down her face, her nose red and running.

No way.

Because as much as she said she wasn't going to break rule number three, she couldn't help thinking that she'd like to, and she had too much pride to stand in front of a man she'd *like* to fall for, crying her heart out because she couldn't let herself.

"What were you looking for when you came back to Spokane?" she asked, because if she thought about things too long, she might decide that the idea of rules was overrated, that only God's rules really mattered and that her three rules were most definitely meant to be broken.

"That's a good question, Goldilocks." He played with the ends of her hair, his fingers combing through the curls.

She shivered, wanting to move away.

Wanting to stay even more.

"Do you know the answer?"

She turned, realized too late just how close they were. Toe to toe. Eye to…sternum.

She looked up, her breath catching as she met his eyes.

"I came looking for redemption. I'd let Jessica down. I'd let my father and brother down by leaving them with the burden of responsibility for the farm and the orchards. I thought my one chance to redeem myself lay in helping my mother keep the farm, but I realized pretty soon after I got here that all she needed was my company."

"So you didn't find what you were looking for?"

"Yes, I did. I was looking for redemption and I found it. And then I found you, and I'm starting to believe that you're the second chance I didn't think I'd ever have." He ran his finger down her cheek, traced a path to the pulse point in her neck.

They were inches apart.

Inches.

And she couldn't move away. Could only stretch up as he leaned down, her arms sliding around broad shoulders, her fingers raking through silky hair as their lips touched and fire thundered through her blood.

Somewhere in the distance a phone rang, the sound barely registering.

"I'd better get that," Chance said, stepping back, heat blazing from his eyes as he turned, grabbed his cell phone from the table, walked from the room and left Rayne leaning against the window, icy cold seeping through her flannel PJs, her heart pounding in her ears, every beat echoing one word, one rule, one more broken promise to herself.

Three. Three. Three. Three.

She'd done the unthinkable.

She'd broken the rule.

She'd fallen in love.

She ran a hand over her hair, tried to quiet her rapid heartbeat. If the phone hadn't rung, would they still be standing in front of the window?

The *phone?*

Before dawn?

That couldn't mean anything good.

She hurried into the kitchen, nearly barreling into Chance.

"Careful." He grabbed her waist, his hands tightening a fraction before he let her go and turned away, the phone pressed to his ear.

"Are you sure?" The taut edge to the question made the hair on the back of Rayne's neck stand on end.

"Any idea how he died?"

"Who died?" she hissed, but Chance ignored her question.

"Any reason to believe that's not the case?" He stalked to the window, stared out into the darkness. "Okay. That sounds good. Call me as soon as you know more."

He hung up, dropped the phone back onto the table, met her eyes. "The police spotted the Mitsubishi truck at a motel fifty miles north of here. Daryl Green checked in there four days ago. When the police entered the room, they found him."

"Dead?"

"Yes. He took an overdose of prescription pain medication."

"How long has he been dead?" She couldn't wrap her mind around it. The man she'd been sure was hunting her down was no longer a threat. Somehow, though, she still didn't feel safe.

"The medical examiner thinks he died sometime yesterday."

"Did he leave a note?"

"No, but the police found evidence to tie him to the bombing at my mother's house."

"I guess that's that, then. They have their suspect, he's dead. Everything can go back to normal." Or as normal as anything could be with two months' worth of memories lost and rules number one, two and three broken.

Maybe she needed a new rule. A fourth one. Like: never, ever break a rule again.

"Kai will be over in a few hours to fill us in on more details."

"What details?"

"The sheriff's department is still collecting evidence, and Kai wants to speak with us both when they're done."

"That doesn't sound good."

"It isn't good or bad. He wants to gather all the information before he gives it to us. That'll make things less confusing in the long run."

"So we're waiting again?"

"Yeah. We're waiting." He handed her a chocolate bar, and she threw caution to the wind and ate it, her stomach churning as she swallowed the sweet confection.

Leon was dead and in a few hours, she'd be free to go back to her life.

She just wasn't sure she knew what that meant.

She only knew what it *didn't* mean.

It didn't mean more kisses in the firelight. It didn't mean spending hour after hour with a man who made her feel like every curve, every blemish and every flaw was part of her unique beauty.

"You're upset," Chance said, his knuckles brushing her cheek, skimming over lips still warm from his kisses.

"A man is dead. I can't celebrate that." That was as much of the truth as she could give, and it would have to be enough.

"Neither can I, but it's difficult to mourn a man who wanted you dead."

"If he wanted me dead, then why did he kill himself?"

"Because he couldn't find you and the police

were closing in. He probably knew he'd go to jail."

"Suicide is such a desperate, drastic act. Wouldn't jail be better than death?"

"I think Leon was a desperate man, and I think that he'd probably lost so much that his life didn't feel like real living."

"I just wish…"

"What?"

"That he'd stayed in Arizona and left me alone. That none of this had happened."

"None of it?" He brushed a lock of hair from her cheek, his fingers lingering near her ear, then skimming down her jaw. She felt every touch, every smooth caress to the depth of her soul, and she didn't want the beauty of it to end.

"Chance—"

"When this is over, after we've spoken to Kai, and we're both back doing what we were doing before the accident, we're going to have to talk about us. Where we're headed, what we both want."

"All I want is what I had before this happened."

"What's that?"

"Three unbroken rules for heart-healthy

living." She said it as if she meant it, but she wasn't sure she did.

"You know the funny thing about the heart, Rayne? It can't be healthy unless it's exercised. Lie in bed all day to keep it from pounding too fast or working too hard and it becomes weak and useless. To you and to everyone around you." His fingers trailed from her jaw, down her neck, skimmed over her collarbone, and she shivered.

"I don't want to be useless. I just want to be… safe."

He nodded, stepping back, giving her some room to think and breathe. Only she couldn't do either. All she could do was look in his eyes and wonder why she was such a coward, why she couldn't just reach out and take what she yearned for without fear that what she'd grab was exactly what she didn't want.

Disappointment.

Heartbreak.

Loneliness.

"I need to check on Emma," she said and did the only thing that made any sense.

She ran.

THIRTEEN

Trouble.

That's what Chance was in.

Big trouble.

Not only had he not kept his distance from Rayne, but he'd done exactly what he hadn't wanted to. He'd fallen for her. So deep and hard and fast that he'd barely known what was happening until it was done, and he was there, staring into her eyes, knowing he'd be happy to spend the rest of his life doing exactly that.

Too bad Rayne wasn't as excited about the idea as he was.

Too bad he respected her too much, liked her too much to push for something she said she didn't want.

He frowned, shoving his laptop into its case,

glancing around the spotless living room. In a few hours, Sydney would have her house back. At least, *she'd* be happy about the way things had turned out.

"Looks like you're planning to move out." Sydney walked into the room, her dark red hair pulled back with a headband, her eyes deeply shadowed. She'd been a gracious enough hostess, but Chance knew she wouldn't be any sorrier to see them go than he and Rayne would be to leave.

"Darren Leon was found dead late last night. Once the police confirm his identity, we'll be able to go back to our lives."

"You sure about that?" She grabbed a coat from the closet near the door, shoved her feet into boots.

"There was evidence linking Leon with the bomb that was thrown at my mother's place. There's no reason to believe there's any other threat against Rayne." But he couldn't help thinking that things had played out too easily.

"I hope you're right."

"Do you have reason to think I'm not?"

"There are lots of things that aren't what they seem, Richardson. It's good to keep that in mind when we're trying to protect people we care about. You have the key. If you leave, lock up. If you need to come back, feel free. Tell Rayne I said goodbye." She walked outside before he could respond and left him staring at a closed door.

She was right.

Lots of things weren't what they seemed.

Lots of *people* weren't what they seemed.

Jessica hadn't been.

If he were honest, he hadn't been, either. Army chaplain, strong Christian, man of faith, but inside he'd been angry and bitter. Angry at himself and Jessica after their separation. Bitter at God for allowing him to marry Jessica in the first place. It had taken him a long time to figure out who he really was, to drop the facade and be real enough to share his struggles with people who cared.

By that point, it had been too late. Jessica was gone.

"Chance?" Rayne called out, the fear in her voice making the hair on the back of his neck stand on end.

He ran up the stairs, his heart beating double time, adrenaline coursing through him as he rushed into Rayne's room.

She stood over the crib, her face pale, the fading bruises dark against the pallor.

"What's wrong?"

"Emma is burning up."

"She's sick?" He lay his hand against the baby's cheek. Hot. Way too hot. "Has she run a fever before?"

"No. She's always been healthy." Rayne lifted Emma, and Chance frowned as the baby whimpered but didn't open her eyes.

"We need to get her to the doctor."

"I should have known it wasn't the new environment that was making her fussy, and I should have brought her to the doctor and had her checked out before this," Rayne said, smoothing Emma's deep red hair, her hand shaking.

"You couldn't know she was getting sick, and the doctors couldn't have predicted that she'd be running a fever in a few days."

"Maybe not, but if anything happens to her, I don't know what I'll do."

"Babies get sick all the time. She'll be okay." But even as he said it, he wondered if it were true. He took the baby from Rayne's arms, felt her pulse. Steady but fast. That was normal for a baby.

Wasn't it?

"Her lips look blue. Is she breathing?" Rayne's panic was contagious, and he felt his own building, forced it down as he bent his head, heard a slight wheezing as Emma exhaled.

"She sounds wheezy. You have her bag packed?"

"I don't know." Rayne tried to dart around him, but he grabbed her arm. "Panicking isn't going to do anyone any good. Take a deep breath, calm down. Let's get what we need and get out of here."

She blinked, nodded.

"You're right. I'm not going to be much of a mother if I run around like a chicken with my head cut off every time there's an emergency." Her voice shook, but her hands were steady as she grabbed Emma's coat and handed it to him, stuffed some clothes and a blanket into the diaper bag and grabbed her purse.

"Okay. Let's go."

"She won't need anything else?"

"Your mom will bring anything she needs. Let's just get her to the hospital."

Chance's phone rang as Rayne strapped Emma into the car seat, climbed into the seat beside her.

He answered quickly. "Go ahead."

"Something wrong?" Kai asked.

"Emma is sick. We're taking her to the emergency room."

"How bad is she?"

"We won't know until we get there." He took off as soon as Rayne buckled her seat belt, pulling onto the highway with as much speed as the conditions would allow.

"What hospital are you going to?"

"Spokane Valley."

"I'll meet you there in half an hour."

"That's not necessary, Kai."

"Actually, it is. We've had some new developments in the case that I think you should know about."

"You've identified the deceased?"

"His fingerprints match the ones on record for Darren Leon. We have our man for sure."

"I'm not sure whether I should think that's good or bad."

"Actually, it's created some new problems."

"What kind of problems?" He glanced in the rearview mirror, met Rayne's eyes and knew that what Kai had to say wouldn't matter to her.

Not Leon's identification.

Not closure of the case.

Not whatever problems or answers Kai might offer.

All she cared about, all she wanted to know was that Emma would be okay.

All *he* cared about, all *he* wanted to know was the same.

He pressed down on the accelerator, then forced himself to ease up. Getting in an accident on the way to the hospital wasn't going to do Emma any good.

"You still there, Richardson?" Kai asked, and Chance forced his attention back to the conversation.

"Sorry. What did you say?"

"Phoenix P.D. searched Leon's apartment after we identified the body. They found $30,000 in cash hidden in his freezer."

"That's a lot of money to have sitting around an empty apartment."

"Sure is. Makes a person wonder why he didn't bring it to the bank."

"It might be difficult to explain a $30,000 cash deposit."

"Exactly. There's one more thing. The evidence team found another $10,000 taped under the seat in the Mitsubishi."

Despite his distraction, despite his concern for Emma, Chance didn't miss the implications. "Someone was paying him large sums of money for something."

"Yeah. I'd like to know what. Too bad the guy went to the grave with his secrets. I've got to go. I have a meeting in five. I'll see you at the hospital." Kai hung up and Chance frowned, unease sweeping through him.

"More bad news, right?" Rayne asked, and he nodded.

"Leon came into a large amount of cash at some point. The police found $30,000 dollars hidden in his freezer. Ten thousand in the Mitsubishi."

"That's a lot of money."

"Yeah, and people don't usually get paid large sums of money for doing nothing."

"You think he was paid to come after me, don't you?"

"I don't know, but we need to find out. We can't know you're safe until we know why Leon had that money. Are you sure you don't have any enemies in Arizona? No one who might have wanted to see you harmed?"

"Not harmed. Not dead. The only person who had anything against me was Leon." She gave the same answer she'd given when he'd asked before, and he knew she believed it.

He didn't.

Someone besides Darren Leon had a vendetta against Rayne. Someone who could afford to pay other people to do his dirty work.

"Who's the wealthiest person you know, Rayne?"

"I don't know anyone with enough money to throw around $40,000 to have me killed."

Emma cried halfheartedly, her wheezing breaths knocking about ten years off Chance's life.

"How's she doing?"

"I don't know. Her lips still look blue. She won't look at me. If she dies…"

"She's not going to die."

Please, God, don't let her die.

"What if she does, Chance? What if she dies because I brought her up here? Maybe Michael was right. Maybe she would have been better off with a family who could give her the kind of life she needs."

"What she needs—*all* she needs—is you."

"Maybe she needs you, too." The words were barely a whisper, but Chance heard, met her eyes in the rearview mirror again.

"She has me, Rayne. You both do." He pulled into the hospital parking lot, lifted Emma out of the car as Rayne grabbed the diaper bag.

Lethargic, pink-cheeked, her lips tinged with blue, Emma lay her head against Chance's chest, reached up and patted his cheek.

His throat clogged with an emotion he'd never felt before, a fierce need to protect that made him finally, *finally* understand just how much faith it had taken Abraham to lay Isaac out as a sacrificial lamb.

"I'll take her," Rayne said as they walked into the emergency room, and he handed her over, wishing he had the right to do more than hover beside Rayne as she signed in at the reception desk.

"She's really sick. How long…"

"It's about an hour's wait, sweetie. Go ahead and have a seat, and we'll call you up as soon as we can." The nurse cut off Rayne's question, offering a pleasant smile and a wave in the direction of the waiting area.

Not good enough.

"Ma'am, her lips are blue, she's gasping for breath and she needs to see a doctor now. Not an hour from now," Chance said.

"I'm sorry—"

"Not as sorry as you'll be if something happens to her because you made us wait." Threats weren't normally his style, but he'd do whatever it took to get Emma into the doctor quickly.

The nurse frowned, walked out from behind her desk and studied Emma's face, put a hand on her back.

"You're right. I apologize, Mom, for not taking the time to listen to your concerns. Come back with me. Dad, if you stay here and fill out the forms, I'll get you once they're settled." She handed Chance a clipboard of forms.

"I'm not…"

"The insurance cards are in my wallet," Rayne said, shoving her purse into Chance's hands. "Can you call my parents and let them know what's going on? Ask them to call Jonas and Skylar and to get the prayer chain going, okay? Their number is on my phone." Her voice broke and she turned away, but not before Chance saw her tears, felt a surge of helplessness.

He took the forms, pulled out Rayne's wallet, copied information, filled in what he could, made the call to her parents, made a call to his mother. Prayed, paced, prayed some more.

Where was the nurse?

Why hadn't she come back for him?

The dark-haired nurse who'd taken her place would only tell Chance that Emma was with the doctor.

Another ten minutes, and he'd ignore the *patients only* sign on the door and walk back into triage area, search behind every curtain until he found Rayne and Emma.

"Chance!" Kane Dougherty jogged across the waiting room, his face tight with concern. "How is she?"

"Bad enough that the nurse let us bypass an hour wait. She took Emma and Rayne back eighteen minutes ago. I haven't seen anybody since. I'm ready to bust through that door and find out what's going on."

"Let's not call security down on our heads

yet. Sit and chill for a few more minutes. Then we'll come up with a plan." Kane patted his back.

"How'd you know we were here?"

"Skylar called. She beat the prayer chain by three minutes. Told me that she understood all about family time, and she didn't want to steal any of mine, but she was a thousand miles away and could I please get to the hospital before she got arrested for threatening bodily injury to the flight attendant who kept insisting there was no room on the next Spokane-bound flight out of New Mexico?"

"Think she'd have done it?"

"I *know* she'd have done it so I'm here, but I would have come anyway."

"Thanks."

"I've also called a friend of mine who owns a personal security company. If Emma is admitted, there's no way you can be here twenty-four hours a day. Worst-case scenario and she does have to stay, he has men ready to run shifts outside her room. Until we know why Leon had tens of thousands of dollars in cash lying around, I want Rayne under twenty-four-hour protection."

"It's my job to protect them, Kane. I'm not leaving it to anyone else."

"Since when is it your job?"

"Since I realized how much they needed someone on their side." He stalked to the reception desk, willing the woman who'd led Rayne and Emma away to reappear and take the place of the pretty dark-haired young lady who sat there.

"Can I help you, sir?" she asked for the tenth time in twenty minutes.

"My friend and her daughter were brought back to triage twenty minutes ago. Someone was supposed to bring me back to them once they were settled."

She nodded, glanced at the computer screen, not even bothering to ask the name. After ten queries, there was no doubt she knew it. "She's down at X-ray. After that, she'll be admitted. As soon as all that happens—"

"Someone will get me?"

"Yes."

He turned back to Kane, saw that his boss was on the phone and paced across to the window, staring out into the parking lot. Much as he wanted to play hero, he knew Kane had made a good call. Twenty-four-hour protection would enhance Chance's ability to keep Rayne safe.

Maybe they wouldn't need it.

Maybe, with Leon dead, the threat was over.

He wanted to believe that.

He *could* believe it…if not for $40,000 and the phone call Rayne had received the night of her accident.

A call from a man she knew to be dangerous?

She'd said she never would have gone to meet Leon, and Chance believed her, but she'd gone to meet someone.

He needed to find out who.

For Rayne's sake.

For Emma's.

For his own.

Yeah. He was in trouble and sinking into it deeper with every passing minute. The way he saw it, though, if he had to be in trouble, this was the kind to be in.

And, while he was in it, there was no sense in trying to keep from getting in deeper.

He walked past Kane, bypassed the nurse and opened the door into the triage area.

FOURTEEN

Please, Lord, just let this be quick, Rayne begged as the nurse readied the second needle and aimed it toward Emma's thigh. The baby wiggled, her gasping cries piercing Rayne's heart.

"It's okay, sweetie. Just another minute and all the poking and prodding will be over." She hoped. She rubbed Emma's arm, holding back tears as the nurse moved in.

"We'll make it fast." She jabbed the chubby part of the baby's thigh and Emma howled, her eyes open and staring into Rayne's as if she couldn't believe the woman who provided for all her needs was betraying her.

"Please tell me that was the last one." Sweat

dribbled down Rayne's back, her hair stuck to her head and she wanted to collapse into a puddle on the floor.

But she was *Mom*.

Moms did not collapse.

They did not melt into puddles.

"It was. She's all set. The antibiotic will help with the pneumonia and the steroid will relax her bronchial tubes. She'll be breathing easier in no time. The doctor wants her under the oxygen tent for forty-five minutes of every hour for the next several hours. We'll check her periodically, but my guess is that by tomorrow she'll be almost ready to go home." The nurse took Emma from Rayne's arms, settled the crying baby into a crib fitted with an oxygen tent.

"Can I hold her until she stops crying?"

"I'm afraid not. We need to bring those oxygen levels up first." She bustled away, left Rayne in the too-hot room, her skin sticky with sweat, her hands shaking as she reached beneath the tent, stroked Emma's damp brow. "It's okay, baby. I'm here."

She hummed a little tune, because her throat

was too dry to sing, and she was afraid her raspy voice would scare the baby.

Slowly, Emma relaxed, her body going limp as she nosedived into sleep, cheeks pink, *lips* pink.

"Thank You, God."

Someone knocked on the door, and Rayne was sure it was the nurse returning with more needles. Only this time, Rayne was going to tell her to take a hike. Antibiotics, steroids and oxygen were plenty. Now everyone was going to leave her baby alone.

"Come in."

The door opened, Chance stepped in and the tears Rayne had been holding back for nearly an hour burst out.

"Shh. It's okay." He wrapped her in his arms, and she buried her face in his coat, hung on tight.

"No. It's not. They stuck her five times to get the IV in, and then they gave her two injections."

"And now she's sleeping. You don't want to wake her, do you?"

No.

Of course, she didn't.

Moms did not wake their kids by having nervous breakdowns in their hospital rooms.

Rayne took a deep breath, sniffed back more tears, told herself to let go of Chance.

Didn't.

His hand smoothed circles on her back, and standing there felt better than anything had in the past couple of hours. She wrapped her arms around his waist, inhaled aftershave and outdoors. "Thanks for coming."

"Yeah. Well, I would have been here thirty minutes ago, but I got waylaid by security."

"Why?"

"It's a long story." He led her to the crib, his arm still around her waist as he looked down at Emma, his face soft with concern. "How is she?"

"She has RSV and pneumonia. I guess both are pretty common in preemies."

"She's a preemie?"

"She was born two months early and spent most of her first month in the hospital."

"So Chandra didn't get to spend any time with Emma at home before she died." He slipped his hand beneath the oxygen tent, brushed damp curls from Emma's forehead.

He'd make a good father.

The thought flitted through Rayne's head and she knew she shouldn't entertain it. Knew how dangerous it was.

"She died three days after Emma left the hospital. It took me almost two months to accept that she wasn't coming back and that I was really going to be Emma's mother forever."

"There wasn't any family who could take her?"

"Chandra's mother is an alcoholic, and there's no one else. When Chandra was pregnant, she asked if I'd be willing to be Emma's guardian if anything happened to her. She asked again the day Emma was born. I barely even gave it a thought before I said yes. Next thing I knew, I was a mom. I don't think I was ready for it."

"But you don't regret it. All anyone has to do is watch you with Emma to know that."

"Thanks, but the only person's opinion that will ever matter is Em's. As long as *she* knows, that's all I care about."

"You're a good mom, Rayne." He shifted so they were facing each other, both his hands cupping her waist.

"I didn't feel like a good mother when they

were sticking her with needles. I felt like I was going to pass out."

"I should have been here."

"That's right. You were going to tell me the story about the security guard."

"Was I?" he asked, and Rayne smiled.

"Yes."

"Here's how it went down. I got tired of waiting for you, and I walked into the triage area uninvited."

"That doesn't sound so bad."

"It wasn't, but when I got into the triage area, I could hear Emma screaming. I ran down the hall to try to find you two, and the security guard took offense."

"Because you were running?"

"Because I didn't stop when he told me to. Next thing I know, he pulls a gun, people are screaming and diving for cover, and I'm looking around trying to figure out where the danger is. Took me about three seconds to realize that *I* was the danger. Another two and he probably would have shot me."

"That did *not* happen."

"It did. As a matter of fact, if Kai Parker

hadn't shown up and explained things, I'd probably be on my way to jail right now."

"Kai? You mean your sheriff's officer friend."

"Right."

"So you got special treatment, because you know a deputy?"

"I got sympathy because the security officer made a fool of himself over a woman years ago. Once he cooled down enough to listen to Kai's explanation, he let me go."

"I can't believe you went through all that for Emma." She wasn't sure if she should be amused or horrified.

"I went through it for both of you. And because every once in a while, my wild side comes out." He leaned down, his lips grazing hers. Just a touch. There. Gone. There again.

She sighed, leaned in for more, forgetting all about healthy hearts and all the reasons why she should have a rule number four.

"Rayne? Chance?" Lila's voice cut into the moment, and Rayne jumped back, her cheeks blazing.

Her landlord had *not* just caught Rayne kissing her son.

But based on the sparkle in Lila's eye, the smile she was trying to hide, Rayne was pretty sure she *had*.

"I hope I'm not interrupting anything," she said, casting a sly look in Chance's direction.

"You know you are."

"Bad timing, I guess. I would have been here sooner, but Fred insisted on coming into the house to help me find the things you needed for Emma, and the man takes forever to get moving." She placed a large bag on a table near the wall and walked over to the crib. "How is the little peanut?"

"Better than she was. Her lips are pink, and her breathing sounds clear."

"She has pneumonia? Chance wasn't sure when he called." All Lila's amusement was gone, and she touched Emma's cheek.

"RSV and pneumonia."

"I've heard about RSV. That's nasty stuff for little ones."

"It is, but the doctor thinks she's going to be fine." Rayne prayed she'd be fine. Life without Emma didn't bear thinking about.

"Well, all our prayer warriors at church are

sending petitions to Heaven and you know I'll be praying, too."

"That means a lot to me."

"When you and Emma are feeling better, I'll take you to my special prayer spot. It's at the edge of the orchard under a canopy of apple branches. In the spring, it's the most beautiful place to talk to God."

"I'd love that, Lila. Thank you."

"I'd planned to stay longer, but I can see that you and Chance have everything under control, so I'll just head out."

"There's no need to rush off." As a matter of fact, Rayne would love for her to stay, because once Lila left it would be just Rayne and Chance and a sleeping baby in the room.

That combination hadn't worked out well before.

"I know, but it's getting dark, and my eyes aren't as good as they used to be. It's best if I head home now."

Chance snorted, but walked his mother to the door, kissing her cheek before she left.

"She's quite a lady."

"Yeah. She is."

"But I'm guessing her eyes aren't really bad."

"Not bad. Worse. They used to be 20/20. Now they're 20/40."

Rayne laughed and Emma whimpered, her eyes fluttering open and then shutting again.

"Poor baby. You've been through too much today," Rayne said, pressing a kiss to her fingers, pressing her fingers to Emma's cheek.

"Is she still warm?" Chance asked.

"Not as warm as she was. The nurse said she thinks Emma will be almost well enough to go home tomorrow."

Her cell phone rang, and she pulled it out of the diaper bag, frowning when she saw the number.

"The ex, again?"

"Yes."

"You can't keep avoiding his calls."

"I took one of them, and I told him not to call again."

"Then maybe he needs to hear it from someone else."

"Michael won't care who he hears it from. If he wants to do something, he does it."

"Let's test your theory." Chance snagged the phone. "Hello?"

"Give that back," Rayne hissed.

"Only if you want to talk to Michael. He says he's been trying to reach you for an hour."

"Fine." She grabbed the phone. "I thought you weren't going to call me again."

"I wasn't, but then I heard about Emma. How is she?"

"She has pneumonia and was admitted to the hospital."

"How long will she be there?"

"At least overnight."

"I'm sorry, Rayne. I know how much she means to you."

"Of course she means a lot to me. She's my daughter."

"She's Chandra's daughter. You're raising her."

"She's *my* daughter *because* I'm raising her." Her voice cracked with the force of her emotions.

"There's no reason to get emotional, Rayne. It never helps. Take a deep breath, clear your mind, focus on expelling the negative energy."

"I'd rather expel you," she muttered, and Chance laughed.

"If you'd like I can write a prescription, give you something to help you sleep."

"You're not my doctor, Michael. Even if you were, I don't need prescription sleep aids and I really don't need to worry about expelling my emotions."

"You're misunderstanding what I'm trying to say, Rayne. Feel the emotions, but keep them under wraps. You don't want to frighten Emma."

"Since when do you care about Emma?"

"She's a baby. Of course I care."

"Why did you call, Michael?"

"To check on you. I know how emot—"

"I am not emotional!" she growled, heat rising in her face until she was sure steam would start pouring from her ears.

"You're under an incredible amount of pressure. As I told you when you decided to raise Emma, being a single mother is a huge responsibility. It's not for everyone, and you simply don't have the temperament to be successful at it."

"Michael—"

"Deep breaths. Just as we practiced. Inhale peace. Exhale calm."

She didn't want to inhale. Didn't want to exhale.

She wanted to reach through the phone, wrap her hands around his skinny neck…

"Let me talk to him," Chance said. The phone was out of her hand and pressed to Chance's ear before she realized he was planning to take it.

"Michael? This is Chance Richardson. I'm a friend of Rayne's." He paused, and she knew Michael was talking, knew she should snatch the phone back, finish the conversation.

But she didn't want to hear one more word about inhaling or exhaling. Didn't want to hear one more word about how emotional she was, or how she was unfit to be a mother. Did not want to hear one more word from Michael Rathdrum.

Not today.

Not ever.

"You do realize you're talking about a twenty-eight-year-old woman, right?" Chance said, then paused. "If you want to see emotion, I'll be happy to come to Arizona and show you some. No. Not a threat, Michael. Just a statement of intent. If you want to be helpful, here's what you *can* do. You can pray for Emma and you can ask other people do the same. What you *can't* do is keep calling." He hung up without saying goodbye and passed the phone to Rayne.

"I can't decide whether I should applaud or be appalled," Rayne said as she shoved the phone into her pocket.

"A little of both will be fine." His smile didn't hide the annoyance in his eyes.

"You're angry."

"The guy rubs me the wrong way. I'd think he'd do the same to you, seeing as how he treats you like you're a ten-year-old child."

"I don't care enough about him anymore to be bothered one way or another."

"You care." He tucked a strand of hair behind her ear, his fingers lingering on tender flesh.

"Okay. Maybe I do, but only because I wasted three years of my life on him."

"It wasn't a waste, Rayne. It brought you here. I need to go. I have a meeting with Kai. I'll be back as soon as I can. There's a security officer standing guard outside the room, so you'll be safe while I'm gone. If you need anything, call. I added my number to your contact list. Use it any time, okay?"

She wanted to ask if he was really coming

back, wanted to tell him that he should, but she just watched him walk away, feeling like a coward a hundred times over because she wouldn't say the words that welled up, begged to be spilled out—*I need you, so don't leave me here alone for too long.*

"Ma'am, please stay in the room." A gray-haired, steel-faced man sat on a chair outside the door, his black eyes expressionless as he issued the command. Stocky frame dressed in a starched and pressed uniform, he looked like a police officer or a military man.

"You're the security guard?"

"I work for Personal Protection Plus." He flashed an ID.

"Nice to meet you." She offered a hand, but he didn't return the gesture.

"Please, stay in the room."

"I *am* in the room." But she *was* tempted to slide one foot out into the corridor just to see what he'd do.

"I'll be here for the next eight hours. If you have any concerns, let me know." He saluted and closed the door, shutting Rayne in the room.

She'd been a prisoner at Sydney's house for three days.

Now it seemed as if she was a prisoner at the hospital.

Not surprising.

Ever since Chandra's death, Rayne's life had been spiraling out of control.

Eventually, it would have to spiral back.

Wouldn't it?.

FIFTEEN

2:00 a.m.

Rayne shifted in the chair, glanced at the clock on the wall again.

Still 2:00 a.m.

The soft hiss of oxygen seeping into the plastic tent above Emma's crib served as a backdrop to other noises. Quiet conversation from the corridor. Footsteps on tile floor.

Even at two in the morning, the hospital wasn't silent.

That should have been comforting, but Rayne felt restless, anxious, desperate to get out of the room. She cracked the door open, looked out into the hall, offered steel-faced-guy a smile as he glanced her way.

He didn't respond.

She hadn't expected him to. After ten or more peeks out into the corridor, she was getting used to the routine.

Getting *tired* of the routine.

Seven hours pacing the hospital room alone and still no smile from steel-faced-guy.

Still no sign of Chance, either.

Not that she'd been anxiously waiting for him to return.

Liar.

She *had* been waiting.

She *had* been anxious.

Neither of those things had brought him back to the room.

Call him.

The thought whispered through Rayne's mind, and she pulled out her cell phone, found his number the same way she had a half dozen times before.

Call him.

But it was two in the morning, and he was probably sound asleep.

He said any time. This *is any time*. *So call him*.

But if she did, it might say too much about what she felt. Might say too much about what she wanted, needed, longed for.

Him.

There with her.

Call him, you big chicken!

She hit Call. Couldn't believe she'd done it.

"Hello?" His voice rumbled in her ear and her mind went blank, everything she'd been thinking about saying for the past seven hours gone.

"Rayne? Is that you?"

"Yes."

"Is everything okay?"

"Fine. I just…" *Wondered if you were okay. Wanted to know if you were coming back. Was lonely for someone to talk to.*

None of them seemed like the right thing to say.

"Missed me?" he asked, and she could hear the smile in his voice.

"No."

"Not even a little?"

"Maybe. A little." *A lot. A whole lot.*

"Good. I missed you, too."

"Then why aren't you here?" Whoops! Not what she'd planned to say, but too late to take it back now.

"For someone who only missed me a little, you sure seem anxious to have me back."

"Maybe I am. A little."

He chuckled. "As I said, 'good.' How's the munchkin?"

"Better. Last time the nurse came in, Emma's fever was gone. She's breathing easily. Her oxygen level is up."

"Then we'll have something to celebrate when I get back."

"You're coming back?"

"I told you I would."

"Seven hours ago." Not that she'd been counting or anything.

"Kai took me out to the motel where Leon was found. I was able to identify the Mitsubishi and confirm that it was the one I saw at my mom's place."

"I didn't think there was any doubt about that."

"Kai likes to be thorough. While we were out

there the coroner's report came in. Leon's death has been ruled suspicious rather than suicide."

"The coroner thinks he was murdered?"

"He's waiting for toxicology reports to come in, but he found broken capillaries in Leon's cheeks and nose that are consistent with pressure wounds."

"He was smothered?"

"It looks like that might be the case. Listen, I just pulled into the hospital parking lot. I'll be up in a minute. We'll talk more then, okay?"

"All right." She shoved the phone into her back pocket and paced to Emma's crib.

Someone had murdered Darren Leon.

Most likely, the same someone who'd paid Leon to kill Rayne.

She shivered, wishing she could lift Emma from the crib, grab the diaper bag and run to some little town in the middle of nowhere, start a new life far away from the danger that seemed to be stalking her.

You ran before. How well did that work out for you?

Not well.

Trouble had just followed her.

Someone stepped into the room behind her

and she turned, expecting to see Chance. Instead, a short, stocky man walked toward her. Dressed in a lab coat, a stethoscope hanging from his pocket, he could have been a doctor or a nurse, but there was something about him that put Rayne on edge.

She glanced out the open door.

Where was steel-face-man?

"How's the baby?" the man asked. Nothing alarming about the question. Nothing alarming about the *man,* but his lifeless eyes made Rayne shiver, and she moved closer to the crib, blocking his view of Emma.

"Better."

"Good. I'm going to take her down for an x-ray. If you'll just wait here, we should be back shortly."

"It's early for an x-ray, isn't it?" she asked, and he shrugged.

"We have a lot of patients scheduled for x-rays today. We're getting an early start."

"I'd rather not wake her, so maybe you can start with someone else."

"Sorry. That's not the way it works." He smiled, but his eyes were ice-cold. A memory tried to surface.

Cold blue eyes.

Fear.

Had she seen him before?

Did she know him?

"It is when we're talking about my daughter."

"Your daughter is ill. If you want her to recover, you need to follow the doctor's orders."

"I'll follow his orders when he tells me about them." She reached to press the call button, planning to talk to the night shift nurse, but he grabbed her hand, twisted her arm up behind her back, slamming her into the wall before she could think or scream or react.

Dear God, help me!

She twisted, shoving her hand up under his chin, forcing his head back just as her brother had taught her.

He screamed, backhanding her so hard she saw stars.

Then he stepped toward the crib.

No!

She dove blindly, slamming into his back as he reached for the baby. Screamed for help as he knocked her back, turned toward the crib again.

He didn't want Rayne. He wanted Emma.

She wouldn't let him take her.

Rayne slammed her foot into the back of his knee and he whirled around.

"You should have just let me have her, lady." He panted, pulling something from his lab coat.

A knife!

She screamed, dodging the blade as it sliced through the air. He lunged again, his arm arching, the blade ripping through fabric and flesh.

Rayne fell, her breath gone, her thoughts fading.

Please, God!

He raised the knife again, then grunted and crumbled into a heap on the floor.

Silence.

Stillness.

Chaos to calm, and Rayne didn't know how it had happened.

Emma!

She struggled up.

"You're hurt. Don't move." Hands pressed her back, and she fought against them, her vision blurry, her heart pounding frantically.

"I said, 'Don't move,' Goldilocks. You're bleeding like a stuck pig."

Goldilocks?

She blinked, tried to clear her vision.

"Chance?"

"Were you expecting someone else?"

"Yeah. The grim-faced guy who's been sitting outside my room all night."

"He's MIA." Chance scowled, helping her to her feet as a hospital security guard raced into the room.

"Everything okay in here, folks?" he asked, his eyes widening as he caught sight of Rayne, her bleeding arm and her unconscious attacker.

"It is now," Chance said, filling the guard in on what he knew while Rayne walked to the crib, lifted Emma.

Okay.

She was okay.

Thank You, Lord.

Her hand shook as she touched the baby's cheek, her head fuzzy with shock and pain.

"Let me take her." Chance eased Emma from her arms, his eyes blazing with fury. He pulled a blanket from the crib, pressed it against Rayne's shoulder, his movements tight and stiff, his hand gentle.

"You saved my life."

"Barely," he growled, and Rayne touched his cheek, looked into his eyes, saw the fear beneath the fury.

"Not barely. Completely. He was trying to take Emma. He would've had to kill me to get out the door with her. If it wasn't for you, he would have."

"He wanted Emma?"

"He said he was going to take her down to x-ray. When I wouldn't let him, he attacked me."

"Do you know him?"

"No. At least, I don't think I do." But something nagged at the back of her mind.

Cold, blue eyes.

Anger.

She swayed, the memory slipping from her grasp.

"You need to sit down." Chance urged her to the chair, and she sat, her legs weak, blood pulsing through her shoulder and arm in wild, rushing waves of agony.

She dropped her head to her knees, took a couple of deep breaths.

No way was she going to pass out.

"Are you okay?" He crouched beside her and

Rayne wanted to lean her head on his shoulder, forget all about her stupid rules and let him take care of everything.

"I think so."

"I've already called for a doctor and the police. We're searching for the missing bodyguard," the guard said. "Hopefully, we can figure out what's going on around here. In the meantime, I'm going to make sure this guy doesn't do any more damage." He pulled Rayne's semiconscious attacker to his feet, snapped handcuffs onto his wrists and dragged him from the room.

"As soon as the doctor gets in here, I'm going to see what that guy has to say."

"I don't think they're going to let you question him, Chance."

"Who said anything about asking permission?"

"You've already had one run-in with a hospital security guard. You probably shouldn't try for two." She put a hand on his arm when he started to move away. "Don't go."

"I wasn't planning to." He pulled a chair up next to hers, patted Emma's back rhythmically as he settled into it, everything about him easy and confident and strong.

Rayne wanted to soak in his confidence and strength, cling to him as she'd never clung to anyone before.

Stupid rules.

They hadn't done her any good. One look in Chance's eyes, and they'd flown out the window of her fickle, foolish heart and left plenty of room for him to find his way in.

Oh, yeah.

She'd fallen for the guy.

Fallen hard.

And she didn't think there was a thing she could do to right herself.

"You're frowning." His finger traced the downward curve of her lips and she shivered.

"You're the most exasperating man I've ever met, Chance Richardson. You know that? Always running to my rescue and making sure I'm okay. Always saying the right thing and doing the right thing. You make it very difficult for me to walk away from you."

"Who says you're supposed to?" He pressed the blanket closer to her arm as several people walked into the room, and Rayne's head buzzed, her ears rang, her thoughts scattered like dry leaves in a windstorm.

"Rule number three is never, ever, *ever* fall for anyone ever again."

"So that's the mysterious rule number three, huh?"

"Three rules, and you've made me break them all. I'm not sure I'll ever forgive you for it."

"Good to know," he said, amusement and something else in his tone.

Fear?

Concern?

Rayne tried to read his expression, but she couldn't see past the swirling stars that danced in front of her eyes.

"You're not going to pass out on me, are you, Goldilocks?" Chance's sharp question pulled her from the edge of the precipice.

"I never pass out."

"How are you feeling, Ms. Sampson?" A doctor stepped between Rayne and Chance, pulled the blanket from her wound and frowned. "This is going to need stitches. Can someone get me a cart?"

Stitches, huh?

Rayne looked at the ten-inch-long gash and the blood that trailed down her arm.

Not as bad as she'd imagined it would be.

She had about two seconds to enjoy the thought before she did exactly what she said she wasn't going to do.

She passed out.

SIXTEEN

She'd passed out.

Something she'd said she never did.

Chance frowned, holding a cold cloth to the back of Rayne's neck as the doctor placed the last of thirty stitches in her upper arm.

"Are you sure you don't want to lie down, Rayne?" he asked, and she scowled, shooting him a look that would have sent better men than Chance running.

He stayed put.

"That's it. We're done." The doctor bandaged Rayne's arm, patted her shoulder. "Keep the wound clean and dry. The stitches will have to come out in ten days. Do you have someone to help with your daughter when you get home?

You're not going to want to lift anything heavy for at least a week."

"Yes. Thank you."

"Good. I'm really sorry this happened to you at our facility. Hopefully, the rest of your daughter's stay won't be as eventful."

"I'm not sure how it could be." Rayne smiled, her lips as pale as her paper-white face.

"Now that you've said that, it's bound to be. I'm going to have the nurse bring you in some orange juice. We need to get some color back in your face." He opened the door, and Kai Parker stepped into view.

"All done in here?" he asked, and the doctor nodded.

"We're finished and you can question the patient. But not for too long. She needs to rest."

"Right, doc. I'll keep that in mind." Kai closed the door, his steps short and tight as he walked across the room, pulled a chair over next to Rayne.

"How are you feeling, Rayne?"

"Numb. Which is better than the alternative."

"Did you recognize the guy who attacked you?"

"He looked familiar but…" She shook her head. "I can't place him."

"Did he say anything, give you any reason for the attack?"

"He wanted Emma. I was in his way." She stood, wobbling a little as she stared down at the baby.

Five minutes.

That's all it would have taken for Rayne to be dead, Emma to be gone. If Chance hadn't gotten to the room when he did, that's exactly what would have happened.

He clenched his fists, the weight of what could have been nearly stealing the joy of what was.

Be thankful. They're both alive. They're both here.

"Do you have an ID on the perpetrator?" he asked, and Kai shook his head.

"The guy isn't talking. We're running his prints through the system, though. I have a feeling we won't have any trouble finding him."

"Good. I want to know who he is, and I want to know why he tried to kidnap Emma."

"You and me and everyone else."

"Any idea how he got past the guard?"

"He parked at the service entrance in the

back of the building, snuck in with a cleaning crew and took a lab coat from the laundry. When the guard asked for ID, the perp pulled out a syringe full of dope and shot him up with it. We found the guard stuffed in the maintenance supply closet."

"Is he okay?" Rayne asked, and Kai nodded.

"Embarrassed, but fine."

"Yeah, well, he's going to be even more embarrassed when I ask Kane to find a new security company."

"You won't have to ask," Kane said as he walked into the room. "I've already done it. I've called in one of the best security firms in the country. Their first security officer will be here within the hour. I'm sorry this happened, Rayne. I'm not going to make excuses, but I promise you that your safety is my top priority."

"It wasn't anyone's fault, and my safety is my responsibility. Not yours," she responded, shivering as she touched Emma's cheek.

"You're sure you don't have any enemies, Rayne? No one in Phoenix who might stand to gain from your death?" Something in Kai's tone made the hair on Chance's arms stand on end.

"What are you getting at, Kai?" Chance asked.

"Our perp had a backpack in his car. It had lots of good stuff in it. A fake ID. A plane ticket to Mexico. Twenty thousand dollars in cash."

"Forty thousand, and now twenty more? That's a lot of money. Maybe I should ask the guy handing it out to give it to me. I'd be happy to make myself disappear for the right price," Rayne joked, but there was no humor in her voice.

"There's a price on your head, Rayne. There has to be a reason for it," Kai persisted.

"I'm not denying there's a reason. I'm just telling you, I don't know what it is. Leon was after me because he thought that by helping his wife, I ruined his life. As far as I knew, that was his only motive. If someone else wants me dead, I don't know who, and I don't know why." She crossed the room, pulled back the curtains and stared out into the darkness, her body trembling.

"I think that's enough questions for tonight," Chance said, and Kai frowned.

"We can't get the answers we need if we don't ask questions."

"You've asked. She doesn't have the answers."

"She doesn't *think* she does, but no one has a price on their head without some idea of who might have put it there."

"Look, Kai—"

Kane interrupted the argument. "Chance is right. Beating a dead horse won't make it move. How about we adjourn this meeting for the time being and come back again when we're all a little fresher?"

Kai nodded. "Good idea. I have a meeting with my boss this morning. I'll check in with you after that, Rayne."

"That's fine," she responded, but she didn't turn away from the window, didn't say good-bye as Kane and Kai walked out of the room. Chance wasn't even sure she realized they were gone.

"Why don't you come and sit down before you fall down?" He pressed a hand to her back, felt trembling muscles beneath soft cotton.

"I don't want to sit. I want to scoop Emma up and run."

"Do you think running will solve the problem?"

"I don't even know what the problem is. I just

know that $60,000 seems like a lot of money until it becomes the value of a person's life. Then it really doesn't seem like that much at all." A tear slipped down her cheek, and he wiped it away, his palm resting on cool, moist skin.

He hadn't wanted a relationship.

Hadn't expected one.

But there it was.

Dropped into his lap.

Rayne. Emma. A little family that needed him nearly as much as he needed them.

"You want to know the value of your life, Rayne? Then look at Emma, call your folks and your friends and all the people you love and who love you, go to church when it's empty and listen to the love God has for you. *That's* the value of your life, and it can't be measured in dollars. It can only be measured in hearts."

"Hearts? Does that include yours?" She pressed her hand to his chest, her palm warm through his shirt. He covered it with his, held it there as he looked into her eyes.

"I think you know it does."

"Maybe I do. I just don't know how we ended up here. Two people who weren't going to fall for anyone, falling for each other. It doesn't make sense."

"Does everything have to make sense to work?"

"No, but how can something that doesn't make sense last? And if this can't last, do I want to risk my heart for a day or a week of happiness?" She stepped back, her eyes misty blue-green and glowing in her pale face.

"Who says it will only be for a day or a week? Maybe it will be for a lifetime."

"I stopped believing in a lifetime of love the day I returned my engagement ring."

"Maybe I can make you start believing again." He slid his hand to the back of her neck, his fingers burrowing in warm, silky curls.

"This isn't a good idea, Chance."

"Then tell me to leave."

"I should," she murmured as his lips brushed her temple, her jaw, the tender skin behind her ear.

"I want to." Her hands smoothed up his arms, rested on his shoulders.

"But I can't." She sighed as their lips touched.

She tasted like sunlight and summer and a hundred unspoken dreams, but he knew a kiss was only that. Not a bond. Not a commitment. Not a relationship. Just a gesture, and he wanted so much more than that from her.

He broke away, looked into her face, his pulse racing with desire.

But even that was not enough.

"You're right. This isn't a good idea."

"What?"

"A kiss in the moonlight isn't what I want from you, Rayne. I want it all. Your dreams, your joys, your sorrows. I want every part of you. Nothing else will be enough."

"Chance—"

"I need to go. Stay in the room, okay? The guard will be right outside." He pulled a blanket from the closet, dropped it around her shoulders.

"Where are you going?"

"To get some fresh air."

"It's freezing outside."

"And it's a little too hot in here. Hopefully, somewhere along the way, I'll find a happy medium."

"You don't have to leave."

"You're wrong. I do. You're too important for

me to risk what we could have for what I want right at this moment."

"Rayne?" Someone called through the closed door and she tensed, her brow furrowing.

"Rayne? Are you in there?" A quick sharp rap followed the second call, and Chance frowned.

He knew the voice.

Knew the impatience.

Knew exactly who was going to walk through the door when it opened.

"Rayne?" Another sharp rap and the door opened.

Fit.

Tall.

Ash-blond hair and blue eyes.

Spotless suit and fussy dress shoes.

Michael.

It had to be.

So much for fresh air.

No way was Chance going anywhere.

"Michael, what are you doing here?" Rayne frowned as Michael walked toward her.

"I was already on my way to Spokane when I called you last night. After our conversation, I thought about turning around and going home, but we need closure, so I'm here. I came straight from the airport. I planned to get here a few hours ago, but my flight was delayed. Fortunately, the nurse was willing to let me visit once I explained that I'm a psychiatrist. She said you'd just been through a trauma and might need someone to talk to. What happened?"

"Nothing that concerns you," Rayne responded, her eyes flashing with irritation.

"There's no need to be short-tempered, Rayne. I came for closure, but that doesn't mean I can't also help you get through a tough time." He smiled the oily, slimy kind of smile that always set Chance's teeth on edge.

"I don't need your help getting through anything, and we had closure. I can't see that we need anything more."

"Maybe you're right, but after I got the call about your accident, I couldn't stop thinking about all the good times we had together. We had a lot of plans, Rayne. It's a shame none of them came true. I'm sure you feel the same way."

"Actually, I don't."

Michael frowned, his gaze jumping from

Rayne to Chance. "You must be Chance Richardson."

"That's right."

"Michael Rathdrum." He offered a hand, and Chance shook it. The doctor's grip was firm. Not too tight.

Well practiced.

No doubt, he had taken classes on how to make the right first impression.

"It's good to meet you in person. I know we got off to a shaky start on the phone. I guess stress got the better of both of us."

"Right."

"I hate to inconvenience you, but would you mind if Rayne and I had a few minutes to talk to each other alone?"

"Yes."

"Thank yo… Pardon?"

"I said 'yes.' I would mind if you and Rayne had a few minutes alone."

"Then maybe I should ask her what *she* wants." Michael frowned, turning his attention to Rayne.

"There's no need to ask, Michael. I don't think we need time to talk any more than I think you should have flown out here to see me."

"After all that we've shared, I thought I should be here to help out while you and Emma recovered."

"There are plenty of people here who are willing to help, and if I really needed someone else, I'd call my parents or my brother, or a friend, or even the old college roommate I haven't spoken to in five years. I would *not* call you."

"I'm sorry you feel that way." But it didn't seem to make him want to leave. He settled in a chair, brushing invisible lint from his dark slacks.

Chance was tempted to pick him up by his silk tie and drag him out of the room, but he'd let Rayne decide when it was time for the doctor to leave. For now, Chance would sit back and watch the show.

He had a feeling Rayne was going to make it an interesting one.

SEVENTEEN

Michael was there.

In Emma's hospital room.

Sitting in a chair.

Acting like he belonged there.

Could the morning get any worse?

Rayne's arm throbbed, her head ached and she did *not* want to deal with her ex.

She also didn't want to deal with Chance and his sweet kisses and sweeter words, or the way she'd felt when he'd said that he wanted more than just kisses in the moonlight. He wanted all of her. Dreams. Joys. Sorrows.

What did a woman say to that?

What *could* a woman say?

Except maybe "yes"?

And she'd been so close to saying it.

So close to something way worse than breaking her rules. Way worse than falling for someone.

She'd been *this* close to wanting everything from Chance that he'd said he wanted from her. Dreams. Joys. Sorrows.

"You're flushed, Rayne. Are you getting sick, too?" Michael stood and pressed his hand to her forehead, the cool clammy feel of his palm making her flesh crawl.

"I'm fine."

"Your arm is bandaged."

"Someone tried to take Emma. We fought and he took a slice out of my arm," Rayne explained, knowing what would happen next. Michael would ask a few polite questions, he'd take a few polite jabs at her ability to handle things on her own, and then he'd insist that she board the next plane back to Arizona.

"Are you okay?"

Polite question number one.

"Aside from thirty stitches, I'm fine."

"And the suspect? Where is he?"

Polite question number two.

"In police custody."

"That's a relief. Of course, if you'd stayed in Phoenix as I suggested a month ago, there's a good chance none of this would have happened."

Polite jab number one.

Rayne almost laughed at Michael's predictability. Only it wasn't funny, because she'd put up with it and him for nearly three years.

"Why do you say that?" Chance asked, and Michael looked confused.

Of course he'd be confused.

He was used to leading the conversation in the direction he wanted it to go. Maybe it was a good quality in a psychiatrist, but it wasn't all that pleasant in a boyfriend.

"She has family in Phoenix, Chance. I'm sure you understand how important that is."

"And I'm sure you know that having family around doesn't prevent tragedies or troubles from happening."

"It's not about prevention. It's about support. We all need that when we're going through tough times, as Rayne is."

"So is Emma," Rayne muttered, but neither

man seemed to hear, they were staring each other down. Brunette squaring off against ash-blond. Tan skin against pale.

Strong against…weak?

She'd never thought of Michael that way, but he certainly wasn't strong the way Chance was. Wasn't physically or emotionally capable of protecting the people he loved.

"Why don't we ask Rayne how she feels about it?" Michael said, his words pulling Rayne from her thoughts.

"How I feel about what?"

"Going home," Michael responded, his smile as fake as his love for her had been. A good show, a proper one, but not the real thing. Why had it taken her so long to realize it?

"I'd love to, but the doctor hasn't cleared Emma to leave the hospital yet."

"I can stay in town until he does. I've emptied my schedule for today and the weekend. I don't have to fly back to Arizona until Monday morning."

"There's no need for you to wait. I have people here who can help me when Emma is released," she responded, wishing she were more like her sister-in-law, Skylar. No-holds-barred. Take-no-prisoners. Say what you mean and mean what you say—that was Skylar's philosophy. If Michael were *her* ex, she'd look him in the eye and tell him to get out and go home.

Go ahead. Say it. Send the jerk packing.

Rayne could hear Skylar's words as clearly as if she were standing in the room with her.

"Of course, I'll wait. You can't fly back to Phoenix alone," Michael said, moving closer, as Chance's arm tightened on Rayne's waist.

"Phoenix? I'm not going back to Arizona."

"You said you were ready to go home."

"Home to my apartment, Michael. Not home to Phoenix. Look…" She took a deep breath, ready to say what needed to be said. Determined to say it. "I don't know what gave you the idea that I needed you here. I don't."

"We've known each other for three years, Rayne. Loved each other for that long. That hasn't just gone away because we disagreed about your becoming a mother."

"Actually, it has. We didn't just break up because of Emma. We broke up because we have different visions for our lives, and because your idea of love isn't the same as mine." There.

She'd said it. Straightforward. Blunt. No mistaking anything. They were through. Finished. Done.

"We're still friends, Rayne."

"I don't think we are."

Michael scowled.

Chance gave her a thumbs-up.

She walked to Emma's crib, looking down at the baby so she didn't have to look at either of the men.

No way did she plan to go from one disappointing relationship to another.

But, then, maybe a relationship with Chance wouldn't be disappointing.

"That's cold, and not what I'd expect from you."

"You shouldn't have come, Michael, and you need to go. We're not engaged anymore, we're not in love and, to be honest, you aren't the kind of person I want to be friends with." She looked up, saw fury flash in his eyes.

There.

Then gone.

But something in her responded, her hand closing over Emma's, her heart pounding.

"I'm sorry you feel that way. I have a room at

the Hyatt. If you change your mind about going back to Arizona, let me know. If I don't hear from you, I'll fly out tomorrow." He dropped a business card on the table, offered Chance a curt nod and walked out of the room.

"So that's Michael," Chance said, walking over to stand beside her, shoulder to shoulder, arm to arm. Barely touching, but even that was enough to bring back what she'd felt when he'd looked her in the eyes and told her he wanted everything.

"Yes." Emma whimpered, and Rayne lifted her, ignoring the twinge in her arm as she inhaled the sweet baby scent.

"Are you okay?" Chance's hands cupped her waist, and he turned her so they were face-to-face. Just inches apart. She could see the stubble on his chin, the flecks of gray in his eyes, and if she hadn't been holding Emma, she would have touched his cheek, felt the warmth of his skin beneath her palm. Tried to imagine what it would be like to give him what he wanted. To take what she wanted.

All those dreams.

All those hopes and joys and sorrows.

A lifetime shared together.

"I don't know."

"I do, and I know you *are* okay."

"How can you know what I don't?"

"I know because I know you." He ran a knuckle along her jaw, and her breath caught, her heart jumping in response. "You're tough and strong, a woman who trusts in God to lead her in the right direction. You'd never let a jerk like Michael Rathdrum tear you down or make you doubt what you know is right."

"Chance—"

"Don't let him steal your joy, Rayne. And I'm not talking about us and what we might have one day. I'm talking about you and Emma and the little family you've built. It's good what you have, and you didn't need Michael to make it that way. You just needed your faith and your love. That will be plenty. Here, let me take her before you rip your stitches out." He took Emma, and the baby reached up, laid her palm against his cheek, stared into his face as if she were memorizing every line.

"She loves you already, Chance."

"She's got good taste, don't you, kid?" He tickled Emma's belly, and she giggled, the sight of the two of them together clogging Rayne's throat.

She turned away.

"She might be hungry. They wouldn't let her have anything last night."

"Want me to call the nurse and ask for some formula?"

"It will be faster if I walk down to the nurses' station." She needed air, needed space, needed a little distance so she could think clearly.

He grabbed her hand before she could walk out the door.

"That's not a good idea, Rayne. You've already been attacked once. Let's not risk it happening again."

"I can hear people walking up and down the hall. Even if the guy who attacked me hadn't been caught, I don't think he'd risk coming after me with so many people around."

Someone tapped on the door, and a stone-faced man stepped into the room. "I'm Ryder Malone from Malone and Cullen Security. Kane Dougherty hired our firm."

"You have ID?" Chance stood, somehow managing to look tough and in charge despite the fact that he was holding Emma.

"Right here." Ryder handed over a photo ID, and Chance studied it for several seconds before handing it back.

"You know what the situation is?"

"I've been briefed. So have all my security officers. We'll do whatever it takes to keep Ms. Sampson and her daughter safe. I'll be outside the door for the next eight hours. After that, one of my men will pull shift."

"If you want to start by escorting Rayne to the nurses' station, she needs formula for the baby."

Ryder nodded, his expression never changing as he held open the door, motioned for Rayne to walk through.

Finally free from Chance and his undeniable pull, and now she was stuck with a granite-faced muscleman who looked like he'd rather be anywhere else.

Wonderful.

Even more wonderful, Ryder stood out like a sore thumb. Several inches over six feet, huge biceps, dark eyes that seemed to see everything and nothing. Did he realize that everyone they passed was staring at him?

"So have you been a bodygua—"

"We're a security firm, ma'am. We secure people, places and things."

"Oh." So much for trying to make polite conversation.

Rayne hurried the last few feet to the nurses' station, made her request and waited while the nurse checked Emma's records. It seemed to take forever, but the nurse finally handed her a disposable bottle filled with formula.

"Thanks. Will the doctor be in to see Emma soon? I'm hoping she'll be able to leave today."

"He'll be in within the hour. He's doing his rounds now."

"Great. Thanks again."

The walk back to the room was silent, Ryder not even offering a half smile as Rayne said goodbye and left him in the hall.

Definitely not the life of a party.

And definitely not the kind of person she'd want to meet in a dark alley.

She had to admit, though, she didn't mind having him standing outside the door to Emma's room. It would take a criminal with a lot of guts or very little brains to try to get past him.

"Here we are, sweetie. Food!" she said, and

Emma shifted in Chance's lap, saw Rayne and the bottle and started to cry in earnest.

"Poor kid. You'd think a hospital would know better than to let a tiny baby go without food for twelve hours," Chance said, scowling.

"She's not that tiny."

"She's tiny enough that she doesn't understand what's going on. People are sticking her with needles, refusing to feed her, poking and prodding her. She's an amazing kid to have done so well for so long."

No doubt about it.

He cared about Emma. No gimmick. No act. No pretending. Just concern and affection, and that mattered more to Rayne than a hundred promises, a thousand dinner dates, a million days spent together.

But was it enough?

He stood, waited while Rayne settled into a chair and then placed Emma in her lap. "There you go, kid. Eat up."

"Thanks." Rayne settled back, Emma sighing contentedly as she started eating.

Chance's cell phone rang as he sat in the chair next to them, and he frowned, pulling it from his pocket. "Hello? When? I can't leave the hospital. Can we bring him here?"

"You can leave," she said.

He ignored her.

"Yeah. I know it's not a possibility, but I thought I'd try. All right. Thanks." He hung up, and Rayne waited for him to speak.

And waited.

And waited some more.

"Well?"

"Well what?"

"What was that about?"

"A witness came forward this morning. A homeless guy who saw Leon go into his motel room with another man the afternoon of his death. Kai offered to let me sit in on the interview."

"So why don't you go?"

"Because I'm not going to leave you here alone. Last time I did that, you nearly died."

"Yeah, well, last time, I didn't have the Man of Steel outside my room."

"I'm not going."

"You can't spend the rest of your life standing guard over me and Emma. You're an investigator, so go investigate. Find answers. That way, when Emma is released, we can go home."

"Actually, I think I *can* spend the rest of my life standing guard over you and Emma." He crossed his legs at the ankles, leaned back in his chair.

"You're the most exasperating man I've ever met, Chance Richardson. Do you know that?"

"Yeah. You told me that right around the time you told me what rule number three was and let me know that you've broken all three rules because of me."

That's right.

She had.

She blushed, but she wasn't going to back down.

"I was out of my head from blood loss. I can be forgiven a lapse of judgment. Besides, that has nothing to do with what we're talking about. You need to go. You're better off out searching for answers than sitting around here." And she was better off alone with Emma. She needed space and time to think, needed to clear her head, try to focus her thinking.

Try to convince herself that she and Chance

really *couldn't* have all the things she'd given up believing in when she'd said goodbye to Michael.

"I don't think—"

His cell phone rang again and he scowled. "Hello? Good to hear from you, Sheriff. He told me. I didn't realize that. I'll meet him there in twenty minutes." He disconnected and stood. "Looks like you're going to get your way."

"What's going on?"

"The sheriff is sending an evidence van out to my mom's place. They identified the guy they took in last night. His name is Kent Mallory. He's a computer tech from Arizona with a rap sheet for drugs and breaking and entering. The homeless guy Kai brought in? He identified Mallory as the man who was with Leon."

"What does that have to do with the police sending an evidence van to your mother's place?"

"The truck Fred saw going by his house the night of your accident looked just like the Mitsubishi Leon was driving. If the two of them were working together, a half hour is probably just enough time for someone like Mallory to clean your computer system."

"Why? I don't even know the man."

"Maybe not, but he knows you. I've got to go. The sheriff hasn't been able to reach my mother, and your apartment door is locked. I need to let them in. They're going to pull prints from your place to try to connect Mallory to the scene. Stay in the room until I get back, okay?" He dropped a kiss on her forehead, dropped another on Em's cheek and then walked out.

Left her alone with the baby and her thoughts.

Just as she wanted to be.

Only it didn't feel nearly as good as she'd hoped it would.

Anxiety twisted her stomach, the thought of a stranger cleaning her computer system sparking a memory she couldn't quite grasp.

Emma.

Danger.

They were the only words she could pull from the black morass of her mind.

She finished feeding Emma, changed her, set her in the crib and played peek-a-boo with her, but nothing could ease Rayne anxiety.

Someone rapped on the door and she jumped, whirling to face it.

"Come in," she called, and the door opened, Ryder standing in the threshold.

"You have a visitor, Ms. Sampson. A Dr. Michael Rathdrum."

"There's no need to announce me. I was here earlier," Michael said, and Rayne sighed.

"I thought you were going to your hotel."

"I was talking to a police officer out in the parking lot when I saw your boyfriend leaving. I figured this was as good a time as any for us to have a private talk." He glanced at Ryder, but the stone-faced guard didn't budge.

"Michael—"

"We dated for three years, Rayne. I'm only asking for a couple minutes of your time. Then I'll go back to my hotel and make arrangements to fly home. As I said, I need some closure. I guess I just need to make sure that we're both satisfied with our decision."

Go jump in a lake.

The words danced on the tip of her tongue, but she couldn't bring herself to say them. "All right, but I only have a few minutes. Emma needs some attention." She pulled a cloth book and a stuffed toy from the diaper bag, placed them in the crib.

"I'll be outside if you need something, Ms. Sampson." Ryder stepped back out into the hall, closed the door and sealed them in together.

"All right. We're alone. Say what you have to say." She didn't even try to hide her impatience.

"What I have to say is…complicated." He walked toward her, and the hair on the back of Rayne's neck stood on end, something cold and ugly slithering along her spine. She frowned and took a step back, bumping into the chair.

"Maybe you should just leave then. I don't have time for complicated, and I don't have the energy to try to figure out what it is you want."

"What I want is to go back to the way things were."

"That's not going to happen, Michael. I'm not interested in rekindling our…romance."

"Is that what you call it? I call it a convenient relationship, and that's not what I want back. I want my life back. The life I lost when your friend decided to make you guardian of her baby. My practice, my home, my reputation. I can't have it all taken from me because of one mistake."

"I don't know what you're talking about."

One mistake?

Another memory surfaced. Emails. Tears. Hers?

Someone else's?

"I know. That's the shame of it. I wish I could believe the memories you lost would stay lost, but I know enough about amnesia to know it's not likely. You could remember today or tomorrow. I can't risk it."

"Risk what?" she asked, her heart pounding wildly as she tried to move toward the door and Ryder.

"Don't." He pulled something from his pocket. Something small, but very deadly. A handgun. Not pointed at her. Pointed at Emma. "If you scream, if you run, I'll kill the baby. Sure, I'll go to jail, but she'll be dead."

"Are you crazy?"

"It might be better if I were. I would have killed Chandra before the baby was born, and none of this would have happened. But I'm not crazy, and even a guy like me has some compassion. I couldn't stomach the thought of a pregnant woman dying, but that was when I thought Chandra would cooperate. Unfortunately, she didn't. I'm sorry to say, you two are more alike than I imagined. Both of you hardheaded and unreasonable. Come on. We're going for a walk. If you try anything, I'll kill whoever is unlucky enough to be nearby." He grabbed her purse, tossed it at her. She caught it, his words echoing through her head.

Killed Chandra *before* the baby was born?

Chandra had died of a prescription drug overdose.

Hadn't she?

Or had her death been like Leon's?

Staged to look like an overdose?

The thought settled in Rayne's gut, stayed there.

"You killed Chandra, didn't you?"

"No."

"Then you paid someone to do it. Who? Mallory?"

"Enough questions, Rayne. We don't have time for them, and I'm not in the mood for answering. Remember what I said. You try anything when we walk out this door, and I kill whoever is closest."

He didn't say he'd kill Rayne.

He knew her well enough to know that she wasn't afraid of death, would risk her life if she thought doing so would offer her a chance to save it.

What she couldn't risk, would never risk, was someone else's life.

She nodded, her heart thudding desperately as she hung her purse over her uninjured shoulder.

"Let me say goodbye to Emma."

"Sorry. We don't have time." He tucked the gun back under his jacket, kept his hand on it as he grabbed her arm just hard enough for it to hurt.

"I hope you're a good actress, Rayne. Because if you're not, the guy outside this door had better be prepared to meet his maker."

He shoved her forward, and she opened the door, praying desperately as she stepped out into the hall.

EIGHTEEN

Chance glanced at the clock on the dashboard as he pulled up in front of his mother's house. 6:00 a.m. He'd left Rayne at the hospital less than twenty-five minutes ago, but every second had seemed like an eternity. Despite the guard posted outside Emma's room, despite Rayne's assurance that she'd stay put, he was worried.

Something felt off.

Everything felt off.

Maybe it was Michael Rathdrum's visit that had put him on edge. The guy had an arrogant swagger that rubbed Chance the wrong way.

Actually, everything about the guy rubbed him the wrong way.

Or maybe it was the thought that someone had been in his mother's house, been in Rayne's apartment, been *that* close to taking the things that were most important to Chance, that was troubling him.

Whatever the case, he'd felt antsy since he'd walked out of Rayne's room.

What he wanted more than anything was to go back to the hospital and do exactly what he'd been doing before the sheriff called—protect Rayne and Emma. Sure, Ryder was there, but he didn't have a vested interest in Rayne and her daughter.

He didn't have a *personal* interest.

Chance jogged up the driveway, passing an evidence van and a marked patrol car.

Shreds of yellow crime scene tape spilled out from a garbage can that sat near the newly rebuilt porch. A coat of paint, a little varnish and the facade of the house would be good as new. Maybe even better.

"Sorry, sir. You're not going to be able to go inside," a female officer called out from the patrol car.

"My mother owns the place. The sheriff asked me to come out and unlock the attic apartment."

"I don't know anything about that, sir. I only know what I was told. No one is allowed in until the evidence team is finished."

"Is Kai inside?"

"Kai?" she asked as if she'd never heard the name before.

"Deputy Parker."

"Oh." Pink stained her pale cheeks and she nodded. "Yes."

"Can you let him know I'm here? Just tell him that Chance is waiting on the porch."

"I'll radio him."

Chance waited impatiently as one minute passed, then another. He was about to open the door and walk inside when it swung open.

"Hey, man. Sorry for dragging you away from the hospital. We finally reached your mom a few minutes ago. She was at your neighbor's place and she let us in."

A wasted trip.

Not something he wanted to think too much about.

"It's okay. Did you find anything?"

"A bucketload of prints. Hopefully, we'll get some matches with Mallory. The more charges we have to throw at him, the happier I'll be."

Kai grinned, but there were circles under his eyes and worry lines etched in his forehead.

"Is he talking yet?"

"Nope. Guy lawyered up before we even knew his name. It doesn't matter, though. We've charged him with attempted murder and attempted kidnapping. If we get prints here, we'll throw unlawful entry into the mix. We've already dusted the motel where we found Leon. If Mallory's prints are there, he'll go up on first-degree murder charges."

"Great, but none of those things will help us figure out why Leon and Mallory were after Rayne."

"No, but that murder one charge might be enough to get Mallory talking."

"Do we know what the connection is between the two men?" Chance asked, and Kai's smile broadened.

"That's something we *do* know. Both men were addicts, and both men were treated for their addiction at Sunshine Acres."

"Sounds like a farm."

"A farm for recovering addicts. Mallory was there two months ago. Leon spent the last three months there. And it gets better. The terms of both of their sentences required that they attend weekly group counseling sessions. Bet you can guess where this is headed."

"They attended the same counseling group?"

"Monday nights at seven."

"So we know where they met and how they knew each other. What we don't know is why they were coming after Rayne."

"Or who paid them tens of thousands of dollars to do it. Or why Mallory killed Leon. There's plenty we don't know, Chance, but at least we have a place to start. Which is more than we had yesterday. Maybe if we dig a little deeper into who else attended meetings with them, we might learn more. Could be Rayne knew a female drug addict, and the lady took offense at something she said or did. She was working at a women's shelter before she left Arizona, right?"

"Right."

Working at a shelter, but she'd had a friend who was an addict. A friend who'd been in rehab. A friend who'd died of a prescription drug overdose shortly after Emma came home from the hospital.

Leon.

Mallory.

Chandra.

Three addicts.

All of them in rehab. All of them seeing a counselor.

Now two of them were dead. Both from prescription drug overdoses.

Easy to get a prescription from a doctor.

And Rayne knew a doctor, too.

A doctor she'd met when she picked Chandra up from a group counseling session.

One thought after another jumped through Chance's mind, spun into a bull's-eye that landed on the one person who might have a connection to them all.

Michael.

The name slithered into Chance's head, filled him with cold, sick dread.

"I need you to do me a favor, Kai. Call Sunshine Acres. Find out if Michael Rathdrum led Leon and Mallory's group counseling session. Rayne mentioned that he did a lot of volunteer work. I'd be interested to know if he volunteered there."

"Who is Rathdrum?"

"Rayne's ex-fiancé. And he's in town. He

showed up in her hospital room while I was there. Said he got in this morning, but what if he's been here since the accident? If he called her from the airport, she'd have gone to meet him. That's just the way she is."

"That would explain why she went out there during a storm."

"It would explain a lot. I need to get back to the hospital." Chance felt cold with rage and fear, his heart thudding as he ran to his SUV. His cell phone rang.

He answered it as he jumped behind the wheel.

"Richardson. What's up?"

"We have a problem," Kane responded, and the tone of his voice froze Chance's blood.

Kane didn't have to say what the problem was.

Chance knew.

Knew he shouldn't have left the hospital.

Knew that somehow Michael Rathdrum had taken Rayne or Emma or both.

He asked anyway, hoping, praying that he was wrong.

"What kind of problem?"

"Rayne went down to the cafeteria to get

something to eat with a friend. She hasn't returned to the room."

"Who was she with?"

"Guy named Michael Rathdrum. He told
Ryder that he's a doctor and an old friend of
Rayne's."

"A doctor *and* most likely a killer." Chance
explained the connection between Rathdrum,
Chandra, Leon and Mallory, his mind racing
in a million directions.

None of them good.

"This isn't good, Chance. They've been gone
for twenty minutes. We've searched the entire
hospital. Neither of them has shown up."

"Does Rathdrum have Emma, too?"

"No. She's with Ryder."

"Tell him not to let her walk off with anyone,"
Chance growled, his blood pulsing in his ears.

He had to find Rayne.

Had to.

"You're angry, and I don't blame you, but
Ryder followed protocol. He checked Rathdrum's ID, he checked with Rayne. He wanted
to escort her to the cafeteria, but she said Emma
had to be under the oxygen tent, and she didn't
want her left alone. She refused to wait. Said

she was too hungry. Short of leaving the baby unprotected, Ryder had no choice but to call for backup and wait things out."

"So he let Rayne go with Rathdrum and now she's disappeared."

Disappeared.

Missing.

Gone.

Didn't matter which way he said it, it all meant the same thing.

Rayne was with a killer.

Please, God, let her still be alive.

"What's your ETA, Chance?"

"I'll be at the hospital in ten."

Maybe less if he didn't get pulled over.

He gunned the engine, pushing the SUV to its limit, a police car pulling in behind him, lights flashing, sirens blaring.

He ignored it, didn't slow until he pulled into the hospital parking lot.

Please, God. Please.

The prayer shouted through his mind as he raced into the building, someone calling out from behind him.

He took the stairs two at a time, raced down the hall.

"Chance, slow down, man!" Kai's voice registered, and he turned.

"Rathdrum has Rayne." He said the only thing he could think, the only thing that mattered.

"I know. Kane called the sheriff. He put out an APB on Rathdrum's rental car. I took off as soon as I heard what was going down. Just so we're clear, your racing down the highway like a fool and killing yourself or someone else isn't going to save Rayne's life."

"Was that you behind me?"

"Yeah, and you're lucky it was. Otherwise, you would have had an entire squad of cars chasing you. I called Sunshine Acres as I drove. Confirmed what I think you already knew. Rathdrum led the counseling session."

"So he manipulated both men into helping him get rid of Rayne."

"Why?"

"If we knew that, we might be able to figure out what his plans are now that he has her. Rayne had a friend who died from a prescription drug overdose a few months ago. Like Leon and Mallory, she attended counseling sessions with Rathdrum."

"There's your connection then. Too bad we don't know what it means," Kai responded.

"Connection to what?" Kane stepped out into the hall, his eyes lined with worry.

"Rayne's best friend was an addict. She attended counseling sessions with Rathdrum." And saying it a hundred times wasn't going to save Rayne. He needed to know how it fit. How every puzzle piece of information worked together to create a picture of *why* Rathdrum had kidnapped Rayne.

"You're talking about Emma's birth mother, right?" Kane asked, and Chance nodded, something ugly lodged in his head.

Something unthinkable.

But he had to think it.

Had to say it.

"This all makes sense if Rathdrum is Emma's father," Chance blurted out. It didn't sound any better out loud than it did in his head, but it fit. Fit so well he couldn't deny it.

"Have you gone nuts, bro? What makes sense about that?" Kai asked, his dark eyes flashing with frustration.

"He was Rayne's fiancé, but that didn't mean he wasn't playing around. Rayne called him a master manipulator. It seems to me that it might be a power trip for a doctor like that to manipulate his patient into his bed. As long as he wasn't caught, what would the harm be? Then Chandra got pregnant, and she kept the baby. Maybe she blackmailed him or threatened to tell Rayne the truth. For whatever reason, he murdered her, made it look like suicide and then tried to get Rayne to give Emma up for adoption. Only Rayne *isn't* easy to manipulate. She must have discovered Emma's paternity after she moved here. Maybe contacted him, asked him to man up and do the right thing. He got desperate, knowing he'd lose his medical license if it was known that he'd seduced a patient. To a man like him, status is everything. He couldn't risk losing that. He panicked, flew to Spokane with Mallory and Leon. Maybe he planned to kill Rayne after she left the airport, or maybe he hoped to talk her out of revealing the truth, and Mallory and Leon were his backup plan."

"If he ran her off the road, that would explain her accident." Kane frowned, running a hand over his hair.

"Why not kill her, then?" Kai asked. "Seems

like a stretch to think he'd just leave her in the car."

"Not really. He's crazy. Not stupid. If he murdered her, there'd be an investigation. If she died from cold and exposure in the wreck of her totaled car, he'd get away scot-free."

He walked into the hospital room, lifted Emma from the crib, and she laid her hand on his face, looked into his eyes.

And he thought he'd choke on everything he felt.

Love.

Grief.

Fear.

Fury.

"It makes sense, Chance. We just have to prove it." Kane put a hand on his shoulder.

"We need to find Rayne. Then we'll prove it. Do we know where Rathdrum headed when he left here? Did anyone check security cameras?"

Please, God, let her be alive. Help us find her.

"Security camera caught the two of them getting into a car and heading west. Same direction as Rathdrum's hotel. We checked there. The staff said Rathdrum checked in a week ago, but they won't grant access to the room without a search warrant. We're waiting for the sheriff's department to get one," Kane said.

It wasn't enough.

It wasn't nearly enough.

"We don't have time for that," Chance responded, his body humming with the need to *do* something. Go on the hunt. Find Rathdrum. Find Rayne.

"We don't have a choice."

"*You* don't have a choice, Kane. You own a business. You have a family. You have a lot on the line. Me? I can afford to get in a little trouble." Chance kissed Emma's head and handed her to Ryder. "Don't let her out of your sight."

"What are you planning?" Kane followed him out into the hall, Kai right beside him.

"I'm going over to the hotel. The police may not be able to get in the room yet, but I think I can."

"You understand that I'm not condoning your actions, right?" Kane asked.

"Not condoning and not condemning?"

"Exactly."

"And you understand that I know nothing

about your plans?" Kai added, and Chance nodded.

"As far as I'm concerned, you were never here. I'll call as soon as I know something."

"I'll go with you," said Ryder, stepping out into the hall and handing Emma to Kane.

"You're on baby duty, Ryder. It's about all you seem to be capable of," Chance growled.

"I don't do babies. As I said, I'm coming with you."

"I don't have time to argue, so suit yourself."

Before either of them could move, a man rounded the corner, walking toward them with an easy confident stride.

Tall. Ash-blond hair. Pale skin.

Michael Rathdrum.

Alone.

"Where is she?" Chance grabbed him by his silk tie, slammed him up against he wall.

"Cool it, bro. If I have to arrest you for assault, you're not going to do Rayne any good," Kai said, pulling him away, and Rathdrum frowned, straightened his tie.

"If you're talking about Rayne, I was hoping she was here. We went to a diner down the street, had a little tiff and she walked out on me. I thought she'd probably walked back here. She didn't show?"

"How long ago did she leave the diner?" Kane asked, but Chance wasn't buying a word the doctor said.

"What diner?" he interrupted, and Rathdrum shrugged.

"I wasn't paying much attention to the name. Some little dive about three blocks from here. She should have been able to walk that distance in less than twenty minutes."

"How about we take a ride down there, Dr. Rathdrum?" Kai said.

"Sure, but I've been up and down the road ten times, and I haven't seen her." Rathdrum smiled, but there was nothing warm or sincere about it. He was playing a game and playing it well.

Chance wanted to wrap his hands around the guy's neck and shake the truth out of him.

"Come on, Richardson. Let's get back to our mission," Ryder said, as he grabbed Chance's arm and yanked him to the stairs.

"I wasn't done chatting with that scum."

"Yeah, well, you keep chatting and you're going to waste our opportunity to get inside the hotel room and take a look at things before the police show up. No way did Rathdrum kill Rayne. Not yet. Any blood or bodily fluid on his clothes or hands, any gunpowder residue, and he'd go up for murder. You said yourself that he's crazy, not stupid. He's planned everything, created his own alibi. Once Kai confirms that they were at the diner and that Rayne left, he'll have no choice but to let Rathdrum go. Rathdrum knows that. My guess is, he stashed Rayne somewhere, and he'll go back to finish the job once the heat is off him. She's alive somewhere, and someone as arrogant as Rathdrum is just foolish enough to think we won't be able to figure out where."

"You've got a point."

"Yeah. I know."

"So, maybe when this is over, I won't knock your block off for letting Rayne walk away with the killer."

"And maybe I won't knock yours off for saying I'm only good for baby duty."

Chance ignored the jibe and the challenge. Didn't care enough to respond. Just ran across the parking lot, jumped into the SUV, barely giving Ryder time to get in before he pulled out.

Heart pounding.

Body humming.

Everything inside screaming for him to hurry.

Time was ticking by.

Rayne was missing.

He had to find her.

He *would* find her.

Please, God, let me find her.

He hadn't thought he'd ever get a second chance at love, hadn't even thought he wanted one until it was right within his grasp. All those dreams, all those hopes that had died with his marriage, surging to life every time he looked into Rayne's eyes.

And he wanted it, wanted *her*, with a desperation that left him breathless.

Please, God, please, *help me find her.*

NINETEEN

Cold.

Cold, cold, cold.

The word chanted through Rayne's mind, chasing away everything else.

She shivered uncontrollably, her teeth chattering as she tried to think past the word, the feeling, the ice that seemed to flow over her, fill her.

How long had she been lying in the dark cellar, trussed up like a prize hog?

Minutes? Hours?

How long until Michael returned?

Because he *would* return. He might not have wanted to get his hands dirty by shooting or stabbing or strangling her, but there was no way he would leave things to chance. He'd come back before he left town, make sure nature had done what he couldn't.

He wanted her dead. He hadn't even hidden the fact, and he'd make sure it happened the same way he'd made sure that Chandra died.

Poor Chandra.

So happy to be a mother.

So excited to bring Emma home.

Dead at her counselor's hands.

Why?

Rayne had asked Michael, but he'd refused to explain.

"It doesn't matter. You're going to die, too, so be glad you're prepared."

His words echoed through her mind, and she shoved them away.

She was *not* going to die.

Not going to freeze to death. Not going to starve to death. Not going to be shot or stabbed or pumped full of drugs or whatever else Michael might have planned for her.

Please, God, I don't want to die.

Don't want to leave Emma.

Don't to want leave Chance.

The frantic prayer filled her mind as she

rubbed her wrist along the cellar's dirt wall, trying desperately to loosen the duct tape that held her arms together.

Blood seeped from the torn stitches in her shoulder, spilled onto the floor, but she couldn't stop. If she did, she would die in the dark, cold cellar. Die, and no one would even know what had happened to her.

Michael had planned everything perfectly.

So perfectly that it might be years before she was found.

If she ever was.

He'd driven her to a diner, made her walk inside, his gun prodding her through his jacket, reminding her that if she tried anything someone would die. They'd sat down, ordered, pretended they were just regular patrons while Rayne's heart slammed against her ribs and the metallic taste of fear coated her tongue.

And then he'd told her to get up and walk out.

One wrong move, one shouted scream for help and the waitress would die.

The pretty cheerful waitress with her white-blue curls and joy-lined face.

No. Rayne couldn't let her die.

So she'd walked outside and around the side

of the building just as he'd instructed, stood in an alley near an old black truck, felt pain like she'd never felt before in the back of her head.

Thought that death had come until she woke up in the bed of the truck, trussed up and gagged and bouncing under a heavy blanket.

Not dead after all.

But she would be if she didn't escape from the root cellar Michael had thrown her in.

She rubbed her wrists harder.

The stench of blood and sweat and her own desperate panic filled her nose, clogging her throat until she started to retch against the duct tape over her mouth.

She'd choke.

Die.

And no one would ever find her.

Sweat and tears and blood all mixed together, and she didn't know where she was, how she'd gotten there, felt nothing but hopelessness.

Shh. It's going to be okay.

Chance's voice whispered through her head, pulling her back from the brink.

She'd broken the three rules of heart-healthy living for him.

And now she needed a new rule. One she couldn't break.

Maybe: Don't ever, ever, *ever* die before you find out how happy breaking all those other rules will make you.

Good enough. Now don't break it.

She slid her arms against the wall again, scraped them back and forth. Scraped and prayed and scraped and prayed for endless minutes.

Please, God. Help me!

Scrape.

I know You can hear me. I know You have the power to save me. Please, Lord, don't take me away from Emma.

Scrape.

Please.

Something gave, the tape snagging, tearing, burning, and she twisted her arms, felt the tape give more and more and more.

And then she was free, ripping duct tape from her mouth, from her legs, trying to stand, gasping for breath.

Alive.

She just had to stay that way.

She felt along the walls, her fingers numb

with cold as she searched for a way out, but the cellar was small, barely tall enough to stand in, so narrow she could touch adjacent walls by stretching out her arms.

No way out except for up.

She felt the area above her head, her fingers catching on old wood and metal. There. The door Michael had pulled open right before he'd shoved her into the cellar.

She pushed, felt it give.

"Just a little more," she gasped, her throat raw and hot.

Something shuffled in the darkness to her right.

A rat? A mouse? Something that had slithered out of the ground and was ready to bite her?

The thought filled her with terror, and she shoved at the door again and again and again until her hands bled and her heart raced and she was ready to collapse.

Another sound broke the silence, different from the first. Not the shuffling movements of a mouse or rat. Not some slithering creature rising up from the depths of the earth.

A car.

Probably a truck.

Probably Michael coming back to finish her off.

He was going to be disappointed.

And he was going to have a fight on his hands.

She searched the ground, tried to find a weapon. Settled for a fistful of dirt. Waited as the car engine grew louder, then shut off. Waited as a door opened, as feet tapped against wood.

Waited.

Prayed.

Listened to something being dragged across the floor.

She backed away from the hatch, feeling for the walls of the cellar as something dripped onto the floor inches from where she stood.

Gasoline!

The fumes filled the small cellar, burning her eyes, her nose, her lips. She pulled her shirt over her mouth, refusing the cough that welled up.

Don't let him know you're free. Let him think his plan is going off without a hitch, that you're going to be burned alive in the tiny little cellar.

Footsteps again.

A door again.

Smoke flowing into the cellar.

Heat.

Get out now or you won't get out at all!

She shoved against the hatch, pushing with everything she had, Emma's face drifting through her mind, the sweet baby smell of her lingering beneath the scent of smoke and gasoline. Chance's gray-blue eyes seeming to beckon her from the darkness.

Wood cracked and splintered, the door breaking with the force of her blows.

Smoke poured over her as she clawed her way through the narrow opening, wood snagging flesh and fabric, trying to hold her back, prevent her escape.

Pull yourself up!

Get out!

She hauled herself up and over the edge, flames shooting up a foot away from her face.

She coughed, crawling across the floor, lungs clogged with smoke.

Black all around.

Outside.

Inside.

Dizzy.

Emma.

Chance.

A hundred dreams she wanted to come true.

Please, God. I don't want to die.

Coughing, gasping, no air. No way out.

Crawling anyway, because she could do nothing else.

A glimmer of light.

A window?

An open door?

Faster. Move faster or you're going to die and break rule number four.

She stumbled to her feet, tried to run, the cabin creaking and groaning around her, fire roaring behind her.

Go!

Go, go, go!

Cold air slapped her cheeks, and she was falling, crawling away from the roaring fire.

Spent.

Used up.

She collapsed. Coughing, choking, gagging.

Barely hearing the crunch of frozen grass, the shuffle of feet.

"You should have stayed in the cabin, Rayne. It would have been easier for both of us." Michael's voice.

Icy cold.

Emotionless.

The man in the doorway of the hospital room.

The car chasing her in her dreams.

Death.

The man she'd thought she'd loved.

She levered up onto her hands and knees, felt the cold barrel of the gun pressed against her head.

"I'm sorry it has to end this way, Rayne."

"It doesn't." She lunged, slamming her palm into his nose, bone cracking, blood spurting.

Go. Go, go, go. Go!

She raced around the side of the burning building.

No time to think. No time to plan.

Running blind in thick smoke, slamming into something hard but giving.

Hands grasped her waist and she screamed, the sound hoarse and feral.

She threw punches wildly, connecting with jaw, shoulder, stomach as she was pulled in tight, held so close she couldn't move, could barely breathe.

"Snap out of it, Goldilocks. We don't have time for hysterics."

Chance!

She sagged, felt herself slipping away.

No!

If she passed out, he'd have to carry her.

That would slow him down. Slow *them* down. Give Michael and his gun an opportunity to catch up.

And that was not going to happen, because Rayne was absolutely under no circumstances *ever* going to break rule number four.

"I'm not hysterical," she managed.

"Then let's get out of here." He grabbed her hand, dragged her through the smoke and out into a field of bright white snow.

She wanted to run.

Wanted to, but her legs gave out and she fell, the sound of a gunshot exploding behind them, snow and ice and dirt spewing up a yard away.

Chance scooped her up, raced for a cove of pine trees.

Another gunshot.

Another.

He stumbled, went down, blood pouring from his chest.

No!

She crawled to his side, pressed her hands against the bubbling wound as another gunshot rang out.

Then silence.

Tears fell, dripping onto her hands as she leaned close to Chance's face, let his breath tickle her cheek.

"Don't worry, Goldilocks. I'm alive. The bullet hit my clavicle, not my heart," he said, and she backed up, looked into his eyes, relief making her weak.

"You'd better be alive. I've spent the past few hours making sure I didn't break rule number four, and I'd hate for all my efforts to be wasted."

"I thought there were only three rules."

"There were until today. I had to make up a new one to fit my new circumstances. Come on. I'll help you up. We need to get out of here before Michael finds us."

"I don't think we're going to have to worry

about that, Rayne." He sat up, his gaze on a spot just behind her.

"What…?" But she didn't need to ask. All she had to do was turn and look.

Michael, sprawled a dozen yards away, the gun lying near his hand, blood pooling around his head.

Dead.

She knew it. Just as she knew that he'd been preparing to shoot her in the back when he'd been killed.

"What happened to him?"

"I guess Ryder finally decided to make an appearance."

"Did he shoot Michael?" She stood up, but Chance grabbed her hand.

"Don't."

"What?"

"Check to see if he's really dead. He is, and it's probably the way he'd want it. Jail wouldn't be a good place for a guy like him."

"He had Chandra killed," she said, the words tasting as ugly as fear had.

"I know." He watched her steadily, waiting for something, but she wasn't sure what.

"Then maybe you can tell me why he did it."

"We don't know for sure yet."

"But you think you do."

"Yes."

"Go ahead and tell me, Chance, because hiding it from me won't change it."

"I think he was Emma's father."

"Michael? No way. He was the most proper, uptight, legalistic person I've ever met. He wouldn't have cheated on me, not with a patient and definitely not with my best friend. Even if *he* would have, Chandra never would have betrayed me like that." Her gaze dropped to Michael's still body, to the blood staining the snow near his head.

Blood.

I have the rarest blood type. AB negative. I like to think it makes me special.

He'd said that on one of their first dates, and she'd been foolish enough to find it charming.

Only he wasn't charming now.

He was dead. His life used up. Wasted.

Emma's father?

No way.

No.

Something snapped in her mind.

More color than picture, more vibration than sound, words echoing into her head.

I'm not sure if you're aware of this, Rayne, but your daughter has the rarest blood type. Only seven percent of the population are AB negative.

Another voice, bringing a memory so sharp and clear she couldn't believe she'd ever forgotten it.

Emma's first well-baby checkup in Spokane, handing her medical records over to the doctor, hearing those words, and knowing, *knowing* the truth, but not knowing what to do about it.

She'd done something.

She must have.

Because Michael was dead and Chance was bleeding and snow glittered in the bright sunlight, stars dancing and whirling as she fell.

TWENTY

Chance dove for Rayne, catching her before she hit the ice-crusted snow, pain shooting through his collarbone, blood seeping down his chest.

"Good catch, Richardson." Ryder strode toward them, his handgun tucked into its holster, his eyes hidden behind dark sunglasses as he checked Michael's pulse.

"*Now* you decide to show up?" They'd split up after they'd reached the cabin, each taking an opposite wall as they looked for signs of Rayne and Michael.

Chance had been heading for the back door, ready to go inside and search for Rayne, when she'd run straight into him, an answer to his frantic prayers suddenly in his arms.

Alive.

She'd better stay that way.

He lowered her to the ground, the sound of sirens and the crackle and hiss of the fire drifting on the afternoon air.

"I showed up with plenty of time to save you and your girlfriend, so maybe you should think twice about complaining."

"No complaints. Just wondering what took you so long."

"Rathdrum saw me coming and took cover behind some trees. We were playing cat and mouse for a while before I finally had a clear target. Unfortunately, he got off a couple of shots first. Good thing the guy can't shoot straight. Otherwise, you'd be dead."

"Thanks for the reminder." He took off his coat, tucked it around Rayne. She looked battered and bruised, her face covered in soot, her hands and wrists bloody and raw. "Rayne, can you hear me?"

"Unfortunately," she mumbled, opening her eyes and trying to lever up on her elbows.

"Better stay down, ma'am. You're not looking so hot." Ryder slid his coat under her head.

"Thanks a lot." She scowled and Chance smiled.

"Seeing as how your attitude is intact, I'd say you're going to live," Ryder responded, his tone gentler than his words.

"I don't have an attitude. I'm having a delayed reaction to stress." Her teeth chattered and Chance lifted her hand, studied the bruised and blistered flesh, the shards of wood buried deep in her palm.

"What did you do, climb up the cabin walls to escape?"

"No. First, I spent about a lifetime breaking out of duct-tape bonds, then I broke through a root cellar door and pulled myself up into the cabin. I don't remember much after that. Just praying and praying."

"I guess God was listening," Ryder said. "It only took ten minutes for the whole place to go up in flames. If you'd taken a few more minutes to get out of that duct tape, you'd have died before either of us could have gotten to you. I see the ambulance. I'd better show the crew where you are." Ryder jogged toward the ambulance and fire truck, his words lingering in the air.

A few more minutes…you'd have died.

It was true.

A few more minutes, and Rayne *would* have died, smoke and flames stealing her life away. Stealing *her* away.

The thought churned in the pit of Chance's stomach, settled into his heart.

He touched her cheek, gently brushed soot from her skin, and she shivered, looking into his eyes, tears swimming in her gaze. "Thank you for coming for me, Chance."

"What else would I have done? I love you."

A single tear slid down her cheek, her gaze jumping to Michael's splayed body. "I…need to get out of here."

She stood and he followed, his finger hooking her pocket before she could walk away.

"Are you going to be okay?"

"I should be asking you that. You're the one who was shot. Are *you* okay?" She turned to face him again, her hand settling on his shoulder, inches from the wound in his upper chest.

"I'll be fine, but then, I'm not the one who was nearly murdered by someone who once said he loved me. That's a big hurt, Rayne. Will *you* be okay?"

"You forgot the part about *me* once saying *I* loved *him*, but I will be okay. Eventually."

"I'm sorry that he wasn't the man you wanted him to be. Sorry for all you've been through." But he wasn't sorry she was there in his arms. Wasn't sorry that their lives had converged. That God had taken two people who'd wanted nothing and given them everything.

"Me, too. When he pulled a gun in Emma's hospital room, he told me he'd kill her if I didn't cooperate. I believed him. I still believe he would have done it, and knowing that she's his...daughter makes it even worse." Her voice broke, and he slid an arm around her waist, led her past the body and toward the ambulance crew.

"He was a sick and broken person." But if he hadn't died, Chance would have had a difficult time not making him pay for what he'd done to Rayne.

"Maybe you're right. Or maybe he was just completely selfish and arrogant. He wanted me as his trophy wife, Chandra and, probably, other women, as his playthings. I think his entire life was a game of manipulation, and I think he got a high out of winning it. Is that sickness, Chance? Or is it just sin?"

"I don't think anyone can answer that question. But Michael's arrogance is what brought him down. He thought he was too smart to get caught. That's how we ended up catching him. Ryder and I broke into Michael's hotel room—"

"You broke into a hotel room?" She tripped, and he pulled her closer to his side, pain shooting through him, his head fuzzy, blood still oozing from his chest.

"We figured Michael was overconfident enough to make a mistake. He was. We found deleted emails that he'd received from Mallory on his computer at the hotel room. One had this address. They talked about delivering a package, so we took a chance and came out here. I think that if this morning's kidnapping had been successful, this is where Mallory was supposed to bring Emma."

Bring her and leave her to die.

He didn't know it for sure, but he believed it, and just thinking about the baby crying and hungry and screaming for Rayne filled him with rage.

"Thank the Lord they weren't able to get her."

"I'm thanking Him for a lot of things today, Rayne." The world spun and he closed his eyes.

"Chance?" Rayne touched his cheek, and he forced himself to respond as pain throbbed through his chest, stole his thoughts.

"It's going to be okay," he said, looking into her eyes and knowing that she didn't believe it. He wanted to say it again, wanted to pull her close, whisper that he loved her, but the world shifted, pain exploding through him, blackness edging in.

Trembling arms wrapped around him, held him up when he would have fallen.

Voices. Movement. Stronger arms and he was flying.

No. Lying on a gurney, blue sky flashing above as EMTs pushed him to the ambulance.

Sirens screaming.

Someone crying.

He opened his eyes, looked into Rayne's soot-stained face. "Don't cry, Goldilocks. As I said, everything is going to be okay."

"Not if you leave me it won't be." She sniffed back tears, squeezed his hand.

"Why would I go and do a thing like that?"

"Because I haven't explained rule number five."

"I thought you said there were only four."

"There were."

"But?"

"We needed one more."

"We?"

"Yes. *We.*"

"And this is going to be the last one for sure?"

"Absolutely."

"So tell me."

She leaned down, her eyes misty-mountain blue, her lips close to his ear as she whispered so that only he could hear. "When you love someone, never ever, *ever* forget to tell him before you say goodbye."

"What about when you say hello?" He lifted her battered hand, pressed a kiss to her knuckles.

"That, too." She smiled through fresh tears.

"Good, because I'm not planning to say goodbye anytime soon, but I *am* planning to say I love you. So, hello, Rayne. I love you."

"Hello, Chance. I love you, too," she responded, her lips brushing his, light and tentative, but filled with the promise of more.

For now.

Forever.

The two of them and Emma, building on the foundation God had laid, making their lives exactly what He'd always intended them to be.

EPILOGUE

Spring had arrived in Spokane in fits and starts, snow melting from the valley first, then the foothills, and, finally, the green-blue mountains. Bright sunlight splashed across the farmhouse lawn, touching daffodils, dandelions and lush green grass as Rayne covered an oversize picnic table with a bright yellow cloth, smoothed wrinkles from its surface and set out plates and cups.

"How is it going, dear?" Lila called out from the deck, Emma perched on her hip.

"All I need are the balloons and the presents. We'll bring the cake out when everyone gets here," she responded, jogging to the deck and taking Emma.

"How's the birthday girl?" Rayne asked, dropping a kiss on silky red curls.

"Mama!" Emma bounced in her arms, her eyes wide with wonder. She might not understand what a birthday party was, but she sensed the excitement in the house.

"One year old. Where does the time go? How about you two come in the house? I have something I'd like to give you before the other guests arrive. Then you can get ready, and I'll take care of the balloons and put the presents out on the table."

"I'll do that, Lila. You made the cake, bought the decorations and washed down the picnic table. The least I can do is set up for the party."

"Don't be silly, Rayne. Aside from the cake, getting ready for this took barely an hour of my time. Now come on. Your family will be here soon, and I know you want to shower and change before they get here."

"I do?" Rayne glanced down at her cargo-style jeans and lightweight sweater. Her family had seen her in worse.

"They haven't seen you in months. I'm sure you'll want them to see you at your best."

"When they were here in December, they

saw me with singed hair, burns, bruises and splinters. Compared to that, this is my best."

"Well, it's up to you, but if I'd ever been fortunate enough to have a daughter, I would have loved to see her in pretty clothes."

"Do you really think that's going to work?" she asked as they walked into Lila's bedroom.

"What?"

"Playing the guilt card."

"Guilt is such a harsh word, Rayne. But, really, it's all about the photographs. My dear friend, Michelle Sidles, is coming to take pictures of the party. She's going to have her favorite framed so that I can hang it over the mantel. It will be hanging there for years to come. Everyone who stops by the house will see us. Me in my best Sunday dress. Your family dressed to the nines—"

Rayne snorted.

"They will be. Your mother and I were talking about it yesterday, and we agreed that we'd make sure everyone dressed to impress. Even Fred is going to wear a tie. Of course, if you'd rather not, you're welcome to come to the party in jeans and a sweater. I'll love looking at the picture, anyway."

"Okay. You win. I'll change." Rayne laughed, sitting on the bed with Emma while Lila pulled a small trunk from her closet.

"Did I ever tell you that my family came from a long line of shipping merchants?"

"No."

"Well, they did. During the Victorian era they were quite wealthy. A few things have been passed down to me." She opened the box, pulled out something wrapped in tissue paper and handed it to Rayne.

"What is this?"

"Open it and see."

Rayne carefully unfolded the tissue paper, lifted out a Victorian child's dress. Robin's-egg-blue velvet with delicate lace filigree on the collar and sleeves, it came with a layered petticoat and button-up boots.

"It's beautiful, Lila."

"Isn't it? My grandmother wore it to her first birthday party. My mother wore it to hers. I wore it to mine. I never had a daughter, so it's been in the box, waiting. I would be honored if you would accept it as gift for Emma. I don't expect you to have her wear it today—"

"I'd love nothing better, but I can't accept this

as more than a loan. It's a family heirloom. I'm not family."

"Love makes family, Rayne. I love you. I love Emma. I think that's enough. Please, take it."

"Thank you, Lila. I know that Emma will treasure it."

"I know she will, too. Now both of you need to get ready. The guests will be arriving in twenty minutes."

Twenty minutes to get Emma dressed into a fancy Victorian outfit?

That should be interesting.

Twenty-five minutes later, she'd finally managed to wrangle Emma into the dress, had wrangled herself into a pale blue blouse and black pencil skirt. She swept blush over her cheekbones and checked her mascara and hair while Emma clung to her legs and tried to balance in her new boots.

"We'd better hurry, sweetie. Your little friends are probably already out there waiting." She lifted Emma, ran out the door and straight into a firm, hard chest.

She bounced backward, would have fallen if someone hadn't grabbed her waist.

"Whoa! Be careful, Goldilocks. If I break you, your family isn't going to be happy."

"I'm not all that easy to break, remember?" Rayne wrapped her free arm around his waist, inhaled spicy aftershave and soap, smiled into eyes that made her insides melt.

How had she ever believed she could follow those silly rules when Chance was around?

"You're pretty easy to bruise, though." He stepped back, his gaze traveling from the top of her head to the tips of her toes. "Actually, you're just plain pretty. And so are you, Little Miss Birthday Girl." He took Emma, and she kicked her legs excitedly, her hand settling on Chance's face. Aside from Rayne, he was Emma's favorite person.

"We'd better get down to the party before your mother comes looking for us."

"She won't. You know she loves when we spend time alone together." He grinned, walking down the stairs as the front door opened and a tall, hard-faced man walked in. Rayne's heart leaped, and she ran down the stairs, throwing herself into her brother's arms.

"Jonas! I'm so glad you made it."

"Of course we did. We wouldn't miss our

only niece's first birthday party!" Skylar stepped into the foyer, her arms and legs svelte and muscular, her belly bulging beneath a fitted shirtdress. Curly hair springing around her glowing face, she smiled, wrapped Rayne in a firm hug.

"Skylar, you look—"

"Whalelike? Rotund? Pumpkinesque?"

"I was going to say beautiful."

"I'll take that," Skylar said, smiling, then stepped aside so Rayne's parents could crowd in.

"How about we move the reunion out to the backyard? A few of Emma's friends are here for the party," Chance said.

"Since when do one-year-olds have friends?" Rayne's father responded, and Rayne smiled, leading the group out into the bright afternoon, watching as her mother took Emma and went to chat with Lila, as Chance and Jonas and Skylar talked with her father. Watching and talking and laughing as the afternoon wore on and friends dispersed and the day faded into spring dusk.

Finally, only family remained, the setting sun washing over their familiar and well-loved

faces, the photographer friend of Lila's unob-
trusive as she snapped photos.

Rayne's throat tightened. She'd almost died
in that little cellar in that lonely cabin, died
before she'd ever known what it meant to really
live. Now she knew, and it spilled out in every
breath, every moment.

She walked across the yard, entered the orchards, the sound of voices fading as she made
her way to the apple arbor and the small bench
that sat beneath it. Lila had shown her the spot
months ago, and Rayne went there often, the
silence of the orchards providing the perfect
place to pray and think.

She'd needed plenty of time for both those
things in the days following Michael's death.
DNA tests had proven his paternity, and Mallory had confessed to his part in Chandra's
death. He'd claimed that Michael had convinced him to kill the woman who he'd said
stood in the way of him gaining custody of his
daughter.

Michael had never wanted custody of Emma,
of course. He'd simply wanted freedom from
Chandra's demands. Blackmail to keep silent
about their affair. That's what the police be-

lieved, and Mallory's claim that he'd broken into the unit where Rayne had stored Chandra's things to retrieve $20,000 that Michael had paid Chandra had only confirmed their suspicion. Mallory said Michael had paid the money to avoid a lengthy custody battle, and that Chandra had reneged on her promise to give him the baby.

It was another of Michael's manipulations. Nothing more. He wanted Chandra out of the way. He'd convinced Mallory to do the unthinkable.

And then, when Rayne discovered the truth about Emma's paternity, he'd brought Leon and Mallory to Spokane to help him get rid of his problem. One phone call, and he'd had Rayne driving to the airport.

Bits and pieces of that night had come back as she'd sat on the bench under the apple arbor. Her anger. Michael's. The sudden realization that he might hurt her, hurt Emma in order to keep his secret.

She'd told him to go back to Arizona, and she'd run.

Everything after that was blank.

Even now, five months later, she couldn't remember how the accident had happened. She believed she'd been run off the road and left to die, but she didn't know. She only knew what Mallory said—that Leon had been sent to the hospital to kill her. Then he'd backed out at the last minute, refusing to pump the potassium Michael had provided into her IV.

She'd been so close to death that night.

So close to death in the days that followed.

But God had seen her through.

Had given her so much more than what she'd ever believed she would have.

She closed her eyes, let the stillness of the orchards sweep through her as she silently thanked God for the day and for her family, for all the things she'd thought she'd wanted that He'd denied her, and for the one thing that she'd thought she shouldn't want that He'd given her.

Leaves rustled as someone walked toward her, and she didn't need to open her eyes to know who it was.

Chance.

She felt him as surely as she felt the cool evening breeze.

He sat, twining fingers with hers, his light eyes shimmering. "I've been looking for you.

Our mothers are having a friendly argument over which one of them is going to give Emma her bath, and I need you."

"I think you're perfectly capable of handling the argument, but I'll come anyway." She laughed, starting to rise, but he pulled her back down.

"I didn't say I needed you to handle the argument."

"Then what do you need me for?"

"Hellos. Goodbyes. Everything in between." He pulled a small box from his pocket, and her heart jumped, her pulse racing.

"Chance—"

"I love you, Rayne. I love Emma. There's nothing I want more than to make your little family mine. Will you marry me?" He took a ring from the box, but she couldn't see it through the tears streaming down her face.

"Yes." She managed to choke out, and he slid the ring on her finger, tugged her into his arms, their lips touching, fire burning, lightning flashing.

Lightning?

Not lightning. A camera flash.

Michelle Sidles?

She broke away, looked into the faces of everyone she loved, all of them standing in the shadow of the arbor.

"You forgot to tell her it's an antique, Chance. From your great-great-grandmother," Lila said.

"He also forgot to tell her that if he ever hurts her, I'm going to—"

"Cool it, Jonas. You're killing the romance."

"You're *all* killing the romance," Chance muttered, pulling Rayne to her feet, leading her over to her family. *Their* family, dressed in their best clothes, their best smiles, their best hearts.

She took Emma from her mother, and the baby grabbed Emma's hair with one hand, reached for Chance with the other. "Dadada-dadad."

"That's exactly who I'm going to be." He kissed her chubby knuckles, and Rayne was sure one of their mothers sniffed back tears. She didn't point it out, because *her* tears were still falling, her heart overflowing as she stepped into warm congratulations, gentle hugs.

"As wonderful as this news is, as excited as we all are, I think we need to give Rayne and Chance some time alone to discuss their plans," Rayne's father, Richard, said over the murmur of voices, and Skylar nodded, taking the baby from Rayne's arms.

"Good idea, Dad. Let's go back to the house and let the moms fight over who's going to give the baby a bath while *we* discuss ways to dispose of Chance if he doesn't make Rayne happy." Jonas slid his arm around Skylar's shoulders, his fingers playing in her hair.

The family drifted away, and Chance pulled Rayne back into his arms. "So where were we?"

"I was saying yes."

"Right, and I was kissing you. There's only one thing we forgot."

"What's that?"

"We forgot to say hello."

"Hello?"

"Rule number five, remember? When you love someone, never ever forget to say so when you say goodbye or hello."

"Or anything in between?" she asked, her heart swelling with the truth of her love for him, his for her.

"Exactly." He cupped her face, his fingers trailing fire down her jaw.

"In that case, I really, really, really love you, Chance."

Their lips met, their hearts beating in one strong and perfect rhythm, everything Rayne had ever wanted, everything she'd thought she couldn't have, right there in the warmth of Chance's arms.

* * * * *

Dear Reader,

Rayne Sampson has three simple rules for heart-healthy living, and she has absolutely no intention of breaking them. A single mother, raising her best friend's child, she knows how easy it is to fall in love with the wrong person, and she never intends to do it again. When a car accident steals her memories, and her life spins out of control, private detective Chance Richardson steps in to help. He's strong, caring and dependable, his faith shining out and drawing Rayne in.

But she has her rules, and she can't break them. Or can she?

I hope you enjoy Rayne and Chance's story. Like many of us, they are flawed and fickle, their hearts bruised from poor decisions and heartache. In the end, it is their faith in God and their love for each other that leads them through.

Shirlee McCoy

Questions for Discussion

1. Rayne spent three years dating a man who wasn't what he seemed to be. What led her to stay with him?

2. What was it that finally helped her see that Michael wasn't who he pretended to be?

3. Have you ever discovered that someone you love isn't who he pretends to be? What was your response?

4. Love means accepting others for who they are, rather than trying to make them who we want them to be. In Rayne's relationship with Michael, was he the only one guilty of trying to change the person he loved? Explain.

5. Why do you think Chance married Jessica?

6. How did that marriage and Jessica's death change his perspective on love and relationships?

7. When they meet, neither Chance nor Rayne are ready for a relationship. What changes that?

8. In your opinion, were their past relationships mistakes or learning experiences? Explain.

9. God can take even our biggest mistakes and make something good out of them. Do you think Rayne believes that when she moves to Spokane?

10. How do their individual relationships with God shape Chance and Rayne's relationship with each other?

11. Rayne makes a promise to Chandra before she thinks it through. As a result, she becomes a single mother. Have you ever made a promise that was difficult to keep? Explain.

12. Rayne made three rules for heart-healthy living after she broke up with Michael. What were they?

13. How did those rules and her perspective on them change as the story progressed?

14. Do you have life rules? If so, how have those rules changed as you've matured and grown?

15. Love doesn't happen in a day or a week or a month. It happens over the course of a lifetime. How do you live your life to reflect the love you have for those around you?